THE LIQUID SPHERE

Original Musical Play

written by

Mark David Gottlieb
&
Gordon Richiusa

The Liquid Sphere

ISBN: 978-0-9829926-3-0

Copyright: 2020

Published in the United States by
Five Birds Publications,
For Heroes' Hearts® Inc.
8112 Terracotta Gulf Ct, Las Vegas NV 89143

This book is not intended as libelous, slanderous or to caste a negative pall on any person or group either living or dead. The story is fictional. How a viewer/reader responds to the opinions or statements made by the characters, therefore is their sole responsibility. We are not promoting or rejecting any religion or belief.

Editor: Gordon Richiusa
Cover Art: J. Shamma McShain
Interior Artwork: J. Shamma McShain
Cover design: Jessie Horsting

Additional Music & Lyrics of *Wheelbarrow Lady's Lament* by Russ Buchanan

BEFORE YOU ENJOY THE PLAY

W e have asked, "What if dolphins are as intelligent as some believe?"

I n the words and music of this play Mark Gottlieb and Gordon Richiusa examine the universal questions regarding discrimination, abuse, and self-awareness with an alternative perspective never before explored in literature.

B ased upon a Dolphin mythology, The Liquid Sphere explores human foibles from a dolphin perspective, and most importantly explains the source of those traits which we believe we share and admire in the animal world, a belief that music/sound not words alone unites all life (including dolphins) through our sense of wonder.

F orty Five Years Ago... (at this books writing) Gordon Richiusa (called Gordie, by his friends and family back then) and Mark Gottlieb shared a love of the ocean and pooled their creative talents to create the essence of this remarkably timely tale.

T his disappointment did not last, as the assistant opera conductor at California State University, Northridge knew Mark's work and expressed interest in a performance at the university. Fine-tuning and rewrites began, but Gordon, (probably fearful of such a success at a young age) walked out during one of those meetings, angrily tossing the script onto the directors desk. For four decades, as a "meat and potatoes writer" (as he called himself) Gordon would answer the question,"What is the best thing you ever wrote?" with the sullen response, "The Liquid Sphere." For, he had lost track of Mark Gottlieb.

F ive years ago, Mark Gottlieb found his old friend Gordon Richiusa on social media and told Gordon that he had kept ALL of the handwritten music sheets, lyrics, dialogue, and notes from the musical director! Remember, in those days there were no computers. Everything was STILL ON SHEETS OF PAPER! The play, in a way, represents ALL people's ongoing search for meaning in their lives.

"What we now have, has both the innocence and boldness of youth and the fine-tuned craftsmanship of decades of writing and life experience." --Gordon Richiusa

"What I've discovered about our work is that after 45 years the magic of our youth is still evident."
--Mark Gottlieb

W hen Gordon and Mark began this project it was purely for the love of the subject. It was always about the ocean, exploring and the moments that brought them in touch with the life in the sea. The only logical next step was to imagine what sea life thought of us. How would a dolphin explain us? The Liquid Sphere was our attempt in that imagining. The intention is that this playbook will be used for its educational purposes for old, young, or in-between to discuss subjects of human interest in a non-confrontational manner. It is also hoped that the audience will have dormant emotions reawakened and that each person will hear their own Dolphin Prayer.

NOTE: A connecting force for both young men was their friendships with other creative people, including friend Russ Buchanan. Because their paths crossed through music and education, Russ was instrumental in bringing Gordon and Mark together (influential, creative friend to both) he has has become a part of the story as the contributor of the Wheelbarrow Lady's Lament song.

It is our hope that this script will be a tool for education, and support the pursuit by young people to express joy. After all, one of the major themes in this play is the belief that music is healing and that young people are responsible for continually saving the world. We thank you.

Cast
of
Characters

-**Young Rogare**–The story's hero, an early teenaged boy

-**Rogare**—About five years older than Young Rogare

-**Senior Rogare**—(could be played by the same actor, but made to look much older)

-**Rowena**—Rogare's love interest and counterpart

-**Senior Rowena**--(Could be played by same person as Rowena)

-**Old Man**—Rogare's Friend and Mentor

-**The Governors**—(who later become the Priests) a group of 4 -5 men of varying ages

-**The Indifferents**—Very strange group of wandering young adults (males and females)

-**Bookkeeper**—Challenged by Rogare for Rowena's hand

-**Rowena's Mother**

-**Rowena's Father**

-**Rowena's Girlfriends**

-**The Wheelbarrow Woman**—Gives Rogare essential information

-**A Wheelbarrow Youth**—Early in play, foreshadows Wheelbarrow Pusher's pivotal role.

-**Young Children**—Playing and singing Dolphin Prayer, in background of key scenes

-**The Teenagers**—Asking questions and setting plot in motion

-**The Townspeople**—The usual variety for both Rogare's hometown and Rowena's

-**Rogare's Young Son**—Presented in concluding scene of Act III

-**Nahia**-Friend of Rogare's Son

-**The Bookkeeper**--a suitor to Rowena , servant of the Priests, and keeper of books

ACT 1

Act 1/SCENE ONE

THE CREATION MYTH
(When curtains open, the theater should be completely dark. The narrator and the conductor should wait for complete silence as well. This moment represents a time before awareness. The following scene is a creation myth, according to the believers in a Dolphin religion. Though the opening narration begins in total darkness, as it progresses, the lights come up slowly to reveal the Storyteller. This is an aged man, dressed in austere attire, stark white or black, of importance later). Lights come up during the first words. He is slightly withered with age, yet he has a powerful voice. Around him is a group of young people, listening. The Dolphin Theme will be cued during the opening narration and will build to a crescendo at the end of this first soliloquy. The first word of
the opening is spoken in darkness, rising from, and eliminating the silence and with great emphasis…(ANIMATION, BACKLIGHTING, AND/OR PUPPETRY—DEPENDING UPON THE PRESENTATION/ PRODUCTION- WILL BE UTILIZED SO THAT THE MYTH CAN BE VIEWED BY THE AUDIENCE).

STORYTELLER'S VOICE
(Lights come up completely, mid soliloquy on the word "Sun" to reveal Storyteller facing youngsters)

Suddenly…the universe began.
A million years before the time of man.
Arising from a limitless space-sea,
From mind and void, four worlds there came to be.
First was the Sun, a source of life and light.
The Moon was made for balance, out of ice.
It was the fairest maid, to Sun the boldest knight.
And, as these two were wed, to be precise,
A third globe grew, and shaped like a tear,
Was formed a paradise…The Liquid Sphere.
Then, again, to even out the grade,
From what was left, our own gray Earth was made.
As yet, however, un-living was the crust.

It was a dry and lifeless bit of dust.
Then, from that Liquid Sphere, that drop of blue and moist,
Great Wondrous Beings arose, and as they did a voice
Broke out of the crowd of newly created things and
Proclaimed aloud...We are the First Beings!

(The creation myth concludes as the music builds to a climax, ending in the DOLPHIN PRAYER melody that will be repeated throughout the story, being sung by the younger children. When the lights are fully up, the Storyteller with his older youthful audience are clearly seen sitting to the forward edge of stage left. Behind them is a city scene of ancient stone masonry and thatched huts. THE SCENERY MAY BE SIMPLE or incorporate costumes with backlit projection screen for animated enhancement, as production permits. One of the youths, who has been listening to the Storyteller, interrupts with a voice that is, at the same time, mischievous and inquisitive.)

MALE YOUTH

Old man...Nice stories...
     (He looks to the others, for approval, but when no one gives it, he continues anyway.)
But, why do you rhyme everything? Can't you speak more plainly?

STORYTELLER
     (Feigning humility)

That is the way I have learned these tales. This is a
human attempt at imitating the singing of dolphins. Next time I tell you
stories, I'll try and remember to whom I am speaking...

> (The group chuckles, including the youth, while the lights begin to
> flicker and change. The Group is somewhat spotlighted and the
> youths appear mesmerized, becoming more serious and concerned.
> The Storyteller commands...)

Remember your dreams...

MALE YOUTH

Huh?

STORYTELLER

> (emphatically)

Listen and remember...

> (The group of youths under Storyteller's spell. As he speaks now, with
> vigor and graceful dance-like movement, he uses the youths almost as
> puppets to act out—and speak--the scene he is creating.)

As you know, from the Great Beginning, the First Five Beings arose.
Delphinus, the dolphin was created from pure Wisdom; the Whale, Monodon
from sheer Strength; ROCKMAL The Octopus from perfect Sight; SCHOON
The Sail-Fish for Beauty and the Shark for tenacity and cunning. All qualities
were part of Creation, but were also the source of some conflict.

Since cunning, for instance is always jealous of true wisdom. There are many stories about Shark falling prey to his own jealousy. He was always searching out ways to test the Dolphin by creating what he felt were impossible tasks, or altering the ideas of the other Great Beings.

(The Storyteller now points to one of his mesmerized audience, who, as if responding to the designation, stands when they are chosen.)

STORYTELLER
(continuing)
GAFF, THE SHARK! (One youth stands)
DELPHINUS, THE DOLPHIN! (Another stands.)

(These two now act out the scene that follows, singing their parts, as the Storyteller appears to direct their movements, as if controlling them by some unseen
force.)

SHARK (YOUTH)
(To dolphin)
Do you not think that a truly wise creature may solve any problem?

DOLPHIN (YOUTH)
A truly wise creature should be able to solve problems that others cannot.

SHARK

Do you know of that lifeless rock of a place?

DOLPHIN

Yes.

SHARK

Do you think that it serves a purpose in our Universe?

DOLPHIN

It seems likely, but to discover the purpose we would need to get a closer look.

STORYTELLER

Which is EXACTLY what the Shark wanted the Dolphin to say. The Shark, in his blind jealousy believed that either the Dolphin would try and fail to get a closer look at Earth, or if he did succeed the Dolphin would be responsible for a great disaster. Unfortunately, the Shark was correct, at least in part.

(The Storyteller becomes more serious and the ACTORS from his audience now have taken on grotesque shapes, giant heads and costumes to portray IN DANCE the following scene, as the Storyteller continues with the creation myth.)

STORYTELLER

Realizing that the Shark was also curious, the Dolphin analyzed the situation and devised a plan to force cooperation between all the first beings and to have the Octopus hold tightly to MONODON, the Whale's tale, to reach out of the Liquid Sphere, through space to grasp the Earth in his tentacles. ROCKMAL, The Octopus' reach was just enough that he could barely touch the Earth.

OCTOPUS

I can't get a good grip!

STORYTELLER

(continues narration)

Though all had agreed that this was the best plan to bring the Earth closer to The Liquid Sphere, for inspection.

WHALE

I'm facing the wrong way to be able to help much. Perhaps I can lift you out of the water a little, (sarcastically) if the Shark and Swordfish would work together to push me forward.

STORYTELLER

It appeared that everything was fine, but then the Whale, with his great weight, could not hold himself outside the Sphere any longer, and the Fish and Shark (probably for lack of trying) gave up and moved out of the way. At that point, the Octopus lost control and the Earth swung wildly through the heavens. First it crashed into the Sun, creating the other planets, stars, and the fiery comets. Then, the heated Earth bounced off the Moon, cooling the Earth's surface, but splashing ice at the top and bottom of the rock, and creating smaller bodies. Finally, the earthen mass came down with a great SPLASH directly into the Liquid Sphere itself!

(Crescendo, Pause)
All of the Great Beings were astonished and motionless, except the Shark who was so pleased, he smiled so broadly, he has been unable to hide his teeth ever since.

SHARK

You've made a mistake with your curiosity, a fool of yourself and us for following you. What will we do with the stone blockage in our perfect liquid paradise? Maybe I should help you devise a plan.

DOLPHIN

Mistake? Perhaps, but I must learn to take opportunity when it is presented in such a grand fashion! Now that we see what the Earth really is, so sad and lifeless, we have a chance to bring life giving water to this dead planet.

STORYTELLER

(Leading up to the next interruption, the Storyteller's fervor seems to lessen and his spell becomes less by proportion. The young audience does not lose all interest now, however, as they had before.)

All the First Beings knew the meaning of Dolphin's words and immediately went about the business of creating creatures, as much like themselves as was possible, both inside and outside the liquid realm. Dolphin realized that, outside of the perfect world of the Liquid Sphere, their creations would not last forever. Dolphin then vowed that when his new creatures would eventually perish, they could return to the life giving water that now surrounded the new planet as long as they remember the Dolphin Prayer.

FEMALE YOUTH

But, old man, are all people born from Dolphins? Are these creatures gods?

STORYTELLER

No, the first beings teach by their example that the true miracle is life itself. The first beings knew they were all special because they were the first to become aware. They were grateful for their luck.

These stories are gifts from the First Beings directly to us because we are from them. Those originals still had a direct connection to all the First Beings; As time passed, our memories become unclear in waking, but remain stronger in our dreams...And, some become storytellers.

FEMALE YOUTH

Tell us a story about Gaff, the shark!

STORYTELLER

(animation will enhance this section)

The Shark was not satisfied with the tricks he'd already played and certainly not with the outcome. So, pretending to be Dolphin's friend, he gave feet and hands to the two dolphins that were placed upon the Earth, in hopes that one day, these grotesque animals would destroy the now living planet and teach the Dolphin a lesson. In a way, all the first beings were responsible for how we are now. We owe the Shark, and all the First Beings a great debt. Without all five, we wouldn't be here at all.

FEMALE YOUTH

How could you know this?

STORYTELLER

Because I remember my dreams…And, I remember the song, a gift from The Dolphin, that we all recall as children, as a memory of the times before we lost the ability to speak without words.

(Children sing nearby…The lights return to normal now, as the mythological creatures depart, and the young people seem to wake from a dream.)

It is good to ask questions. That is a very Dolphin thing for you to do. Delphinus' great gift to humans is a desire to seek joy and appreciate life beyond words.

(The Storyteller watches children come into view and while they play they begin to sing,

"La, La, La, La, LaLa, LaLa, La La La La, la la la, this causes the Storyteller to begin to chant along with the children, then whistle and then hum the haunting melody of the Dolphin Prayer. The youth join him, along with the music that builds to the first full orchestration of this haunting melody. This production number ends with just the simple melody and voices of the chorus without instruments. A group has reformed around the Old Storyteller…He continues)

STORYTELLER

There was a time before now, when things were not perfect. People were not allowed to think and believe as they wished, or to ask questions as you have…

FEMALE YOUTH

What happened to make our world the way it is today? Why were children not allowed to sing their songs? Why do you continue to tell us these stories now?
Why…

WHEELBARROW WOMAN

(A young woman wheels a wheelbarrow across the stage, hears the female youths question, comments and moves on…not waiting for a response. Everyone waits almost reverently.)
Why do you continue to ask all these great questions?

STORYTELLER

Things have not always been as they are now. Some had to suffer for what we now take for granted. Storytellers were not even allowed, though they were just humans who could still hear the Dolphin Song clearly. Everyone retains qualities of all the First Beings. We were all born with the song of the Dolphin. It was a gift, from Delphinus, our connection to The Liquid Sphere, a way to get back home when this life ends.

YOUTH

Do some people not hear the song?

STORYTELLER

At one time there were many who were born without even a remnant of the Dolphin Prayer. Their dreams were empty, silent. Not only was it absent from their dreams but the singing of our Dolphin Prayer or the telling of our Stories was forbidden. While the singing of children was only mildly tolerated, any expression of the Song by adults was punishable by death. Would you like to hear another story about some of those first humans, a young person much like yourself? His name was Rogare, The One Who Wonders…

END SCENE

IMPORTANT NOTE on stage direction: (In the first act, and at the beginning of the second, this set, the Storyteller and Youths will be off to the side of the stage, or animated in such a way as to show that they are NOT part of the story being told.)

(The "story" being told now opens in a square where Rogare is defending the Old Man.)

ACT One/
SCENE TWO

ROGARE

(a young man)
But, you're not listening. You're not giving him a chance! He's not trying to change YOU. His stories can't hurt you!

GOVERNOR LEADER

Do I look afraid of an old man stories?

ROGARE

I didn't say that!

GOVERNOR LEADER

Who are YOU?

ROGARE

(frightened, bowing his head. NOTE to ACTOR: SIGNIFICANT LINE. Don't throw it away!)
Me? My name? My name…is nothing…

GOVERNOR 2

(Speaking to the first governor, brushing Rogare aside…)
We don't want to give him any chances. This type of gathering never leads to any good. It has been forbidden.

GOVERNOR 3

We don't take orders from the sea or any creatures in it. Tales of a Liquid Sphere or Heaven in the ocean! It's crazy talk that takes away from the common goals and good. We've been asked to set some standards. We don't do this for our own sakes, but for yours.
(The crowd grumbles, grows restless, but does not move against The Old Man or Rogare…Rogare moves himself between the Governor and the old man, as a precaution to possible danger.)

GOVERNOR LEADER

We've been generous until now…We could punish the children when they sing their meaningless song but we allow that. And until now we've allowed you to tell your wild tales. But that ENDS NOW!

GOVERNOR LEADER

(turning to the old man directly)

And YOU [looking at the old man] you're supposed to be an example at your age, not acting like a child, believing in fairy tales!

ROGARE

I promise he won't cause any more problems. I promise!

(This seems to take the edge off the crowd, and the Governor fidgets uncomfortably, realizing he can't take his venom any further at this time.)

GOVERNOR

All right then! He's YOUR responsibility. But, if there is one more violation YOU will both be punished.

(The crowd leaves abruptly, leaving the old man and Rogare alone on stage. Rogare looks after the crowd, and the old man, seemingly unconcerned with what just happened, speaks to Rogare's back.)

OLD MAN

Why do you risk your safety for me Rogare?

ROGARE

(Rogare turns to the question).

You know why. When I lost both my parents, and others saw me as strange and different, you took me in. Why did you do that?

OLD MAN

I can see myself in you. You and I are the same.

ROGARE

Yes, we're both going to end up very sorry…probably dead because of a myth, a dream and a song…

(both smile, scoff and shake their heads as if amused at the absurdity.)

OLD MAN

That's why you should leave as soon as possible.

ROGARE

Leave? Who'll take care of you?

OLD MAN

And, just a minute ago I was worrying about taking care of you!
Do you still hear the song and have the dreams?

ROGARE

Yes, I have the dreams and I hear the song both waking and sleeping.

OLD MAN

The Governors seem not to hear the song, if they've ever heard it at all. And, their dreams are for sleeping and forgetting, not for waking... or believing.

ROGARE

(having an idea that he doesn't believe is true)
Couldn't you just stop telling the stories?

OLD MAN

No more than you can stop hearing the song.

ROGARE

(Resignedly)
But, I can't protect you forever.

OLD MAN

You mean you can't protect me much longer.

ROGARE

(smiling again)
How did I give myself away, then? How long have you known?

OLD MAN

How long have I known that you WANT to leave this place? That you are only staying out of a sense of duty to me?

ROGARE

Yes.

OLD MAN

Well, this is the first time I've heard of it! But, at least I am relieved to know that we are of the same mind. It's not safe for you here.
(Both Laugh)

ROGARE

You tricky old shark! You are a cunning one...

OLD MAN
(Musical cue over the next few lines of dialogue)
Why do you feel you must you go?

ROGARE
I'm like Delphinus; I need to see for myself. I want to know…"

OLD MAN
What do you want to know?

ROGARE
I just want to know. I want to see if what I believe to be true IS true.

I want to find others like us who, perhaps know more about
our beginning or our end…Who hear the same
Song, who have the same dreams….

(Music interrupts as the following song begins…solo by Rogare.)
ROGARE, THE ONE WHO WONDERS
ROGARE
ROGARE, ONE WHO WONDERS.
I WANT TO KNOW.
TELL ME WHAT IT THE RIGHT WAY?
WHERE SHOULD I GO?
SEARCHING AND PLEADING FOR ANSWERS TO
QUESTIONS.
BUT ARE THERE NO ANSWERS AS ALL?
ACHING, HOW LARGE IS THE UNIVERSE?
WONDER HOW SMALL?
DARE I DEFY THE UNIVERSE?
SHOULD I STAND TALL"
LAUNCHING MYSELF LIKE A SPEAR TOWARDS
AN ANSWER BUT ARE THERE NOT ANSWERS
AT ALL?
I REMEMBER FATHER GROWING OLD.
AND WHEN HE LEFT WHERE DID HE GO?
MOTHER'S HANDS WORKED BARE TO FEED US.
ALWAYS WARM AND ALWAYS SMILING.
MY HEART YEARNS TO KNOW IT'S MEANING.
WHO AM I? WHERE AM I GOING?
I HAVE SEEN NOTHING YET!
NOTHING AT ALL!

DOLPHINUS TELL ME WHEN…
TELL ME WHEN WILL MY JOURNEY BEGIN.
ROGARE, ONE WHO WONDERS.
I WANT TO KNOW.
TELL ME WHAT IT THE RIGHT WAY?
WHERE SHOULD I GO?
LAUNCHING MYSELF LIKE A SPEAR TOWARDS
AN ANSWER BUT ARE THERE NO ANSWERS?
ARE THERE NO ANSWERS?
ARE THERE NO ANSWERS, AT ALL?

(Sensing Rogare's pain old man seeks to comfort the boy…the old man sings his solo…)

OLD MAN

ROGARE, NO!
ROGARE, THERE'LL COME A TIME WHEN THEIR
SONG WILL RETURN TO YOU.
ROGARE, YOU MUST NOT MOURN YOUR LEAVING,
YOUR CHILDHOOD'S END.
CAN YOU SEE?
THERE ARE PEOPLE HERE WHO KNOW YOUR
YEARNING.
QUIET BOY, THOUGH I KNOW YOUR HEART

WILL GROW MUCH STRONGER WHEN THEIR
SONG RETURNS.
ROGARE, YOU MUST NOT FEEL SAD AS YOUR
JOURNEY BEGINS.
YOU ARE NOT ALONE.
AND YOU MUST NOT BE SADDENED WHEN
YOUR BRIGHT EYES SEE WHAT AWAITS.
ROGARE, LOOK!!
CAN'T YOU SEE THE BEAUTY THAT SURROUNDS YOU?
DO YOU HEAR THEIR SWEET VOICES SINGING TO THE
HEAVENS, TO THE LIQUID SPHERE?
(In the distance the sounds of young children singing the dolphin
Prayer can be heard)

ROGARE, THERE WAS A TIME WHEN YOU WERE YOUNG
YOU HEARD A SONG IN YOUR HEART.
IT IS A REMNANT OF THEIR GIFT.
AND THROUGH THIS SONG, THIS PRAYER, THAT
DOPHINUS HAS GIVEN US
WE CAN BE SURE WE'LL FIND OUR WAY BACK HOME.
(As the sound of the children singing becomes louder old man
Cries out excitedly…)
LISTEN! LISTEN! DO YOU HEAR?
WHERE ARE THE CHILDREN?
LET'S CALL THE CHILDREN1
CHILDREN, OH CHILDREN!
COME AND LISTEN TO YOUR ELDERS.
CHILDREN, OH CHILDREN!
NOW'S THE TIME TO ASK YOUR ELDERS
ALL THE QUESTIONS THAT ARE TEARING.
IN THE END THE OLD WILL SHOW
THAT THE THINGS THAT YOU ARE FEARING
ARE THE THINGS THAT YOU DON'T KNOW!

CHILDREN
WE FEAR THE DARKNESS LATE AT NIGHT.

OLD MAN
WELL I FEAR THE DARKNESS TOO.

CHILDREN
WE MISS OUR LOVED ONES WHEN THEY'VE GONE.

OLD MAN

WELL, I MISS MY LOVED ONES TOO.

CHILDREN

WHEN WE'RE SCARED WE RUN AND HIDE AWAY.

OLD MAN

WHEN WE'RE HURT WE ALL FEEL PAIN.

CHILDREN

ARE WE ALL THE SAME INSIDE. TELL ME!

OLD MAN

YES, THOUGH WE ALL MAY CHANGE WITH TIME.
(TO HIMSELF..) CHANGE WITH TIME.

CHILDREN

ALL TOGETHER, ALL TOGETHER.
WE'RE MUCH STRONGER THAN APART.
ALL TOGETHER, ALL TOGETHER.

OLD MAN

COME I'LL LET YOU TOUCH MY HEART.
THIS IS JUST THE PLACE TO START.

CHILDREN

ALL TOGETHER, ALL TOGETHER,
DELPHINUS IS IN OUR DREAMS.
ALL TOGETHER, ALL TOGETHER.

OLD MAN

I KNOW THAT IS HOW IT SEEMS.
WHAT DO YOU ALL THINK IT MEANS?

CHILDREN

THERE'S A SONG THAT WE WERE BORN WITH
IF WE SING IT LOUD AND TRUE
THERE'S A SONG THAT WE WERE BORN WITH.

OLD MAN

DELPHINUS, THE LIQUID SPHERE.
SING IT LOUD IT TAKES YOU THERE.
(At this point in the song which is building to a frenzy the children, in the

throes of joy and shared excitement grab OLD MAN'S as they begin to
dance wildly, spinning him around and round..)
OH NO! I'M MUCH TOO OLD. (laughing playfully)
YES! LIKE THAT! (Etc. As they dance together…)

LA LA LA LA LA LA LA LA ….

CHILDREN

NO PLACE TOO HIGH.
NO LAND THAT'S TOO FAR.
WE'RE ON OUR WAY HOME. LIQUID SPHERE.
ALL TOGETHER WHO DO WE SING FOR?
WHO DO WE SING FOR?
DELPHINUS! DELPHINUS!
ALL TOGETHER WHO DO WE SING FOR?
WHO DO WE SING FOR?
DELPHINUS! DELPHINUS!
DELPHINUS! DELPHINUS!
(At the height of joy and ecstasy all come to the front of the stage, OLD
MAN,
CHILDREN, as ROGARE watch mesmerized)

CHILDREN and OLD MAN
(Singing loudly and in reverence the DOLPHIN PRAYER—no words, just
sounds and emotion.)
(Chorus exits quickly.)

END SCENE

Act One/SCENE 3

(At The Old Man's House, when lights come up, a large doorway gives the appearance of a room. Rogare and the Old Man are on one side of the door. Rogare listens close to the door and seems anxious.)

ROGARE

What did you do? What did you do?

OLD MAN

You will need to leave right away…
It's no longer safe for you to be seen with me.

ROGARE

How can I leave you? I CAN'T leave you.
(He looks at the old man and it is obvious that Rogare is in complete turmoil.)

OLD MAN

Rogare, you have to leave. You heard what they said.
(Music begins and Rogare is not given a chance to finish his words. He looks at
the Old Man and a strange smiling, yet glaring appearance has come over him.)

ROGARE

What is it? (looks around nervously) Are you alright?
(Rogare begins to move toward the Old Man, but his progress is noticeably difficult and strained. The Old Man begins to sing as if hearing or seeing something that Rogare cannot. This dialogue is led, musically into the next lyrics…)

OLD MAN

I'M FEELING SOMETHING. IT'S WARM AND NICE.
GOVERNORS
(In unison, from outside the door, sing their part unintelligibly.)
AHHH AHHHH AHHH, AHH AHHHH, AHHH, AHHH AHHH AHHH
AHHHH.

OLD MAN

THE WORD ITSELF THOUGH, IS COLD AS ICE.

GOVERNORS
(They sing words now in the same pattern as the previous sounds.)
WHERE ARE YOU? WHERE IS HE? BREAK DOWN THE DOOR!

OLD MAN
(Unaffected by the GOVERNOR, who are just outside, Old Man continues.)
END OF LIFE, FLOWING GENTLY TO ME
MERE WORDS CAN'T SAY WHAT I SEE.
THERE'S A PLACE, WHERE THERE'S NO RIGHT OR WRONG
JUST LIKE I'VE KNOWN ALL ALONG.
THE LIQUID SHPERE IS CALLING, LIKE ENDLESS BREATH.

GOVERNORS
(breaking in)
MUST STOP HIM! DON'T LISTEN! PLUG YOUR EARS!

OLD MAN
BUT, TO REACH THAT PLACE THERE…I MUST KNOW DEATH.

GOVERNORS
LOOK AT HIM! BEWITCHING THIS POOR BOY WITH HIS LIES OF
DOLPHINS
AS MEN'S GODS AND LIQUID SPHERES!

OLD MAN
(To Rogare entirely, seeming to ignore the intruders.)
COME CLOSER NOW MY YOUNG FRIEND, AND WITNESS LIFE
COMPLETELY.

GOVERNORS
(To one another)
DON'T LOOK NOW. TURN YOUR HEADS!

OLD MAN
IT COMES TO ALL IN THE END.
WHEN YOURS COME, TASTE IT SWEETLY.

GOVERNORS
(Gaining strength from desperation.)
DEATH'S NOT SWEET! DEATH TASTES BAD.
DID YOU HEAR WHAT HE SAID?
THAT THERE IS BEAUTY IN BEING DEAD?
HE MUST BE MAD!

OLD MAN
WHEN I'M GONE, DO NOT FEEL SAD FOR MY LOSS.
I'M NOT DONE: I'VE ONLY BEEN CHANGED
BY WHAT YOU LOOK FOR NOW; I'LL BE REARRANGED
BY DEATH. AND IT'S WORTH THE COST!
 (Slow motion surrealistic air pervades the stage as the Old Man is taken by the
GOVERNOR, and bound while Rogare looks on in horror. There are a few measures at the end of this scene where there is a counterpoint between the GOVERNORS, Rogare and Old Man.)

ROGARE
WHAT I SEE? MAD DREAMS!
CAN IT BE AS HE SAID?
CAN I LEARN OF SUCH THINGS?
TO SEE JOY IN THESE SCHEMES OF THE DEAD?
DELPHENIS, PLEASE, IF YOU ARE THERE…
UNFOLD THE TRUTH TO ME,
THE BEAUTY THERE.
HE SAYS TRUTH, BUT THEY SAY LIES,
NOW HE DIES!

GOVERNORS (Mocking Rogare)
DELPHENIS, PLEASE, IF YOU ARE THERE…
UNFOLD THE TRUTH TO ME,
THE BEAUTY THERE.
HE SAYS TRUTH, BUT THEY SAY LIES

ROGARE
WILL I DWELL WITHIN THE LIQUID SPHERE?
WHEN DEATH COMES TO ME NOW, BUT I HEAR:
HE SAYS JOY, THEY SAY PAIN.
IS HE REALLY INSANE?
WORLD IS SPINNING, SO'S MY MIND.
A SIGHT LIKE THIS COULD LEAD THE BLIND ASTRAY.
SHOULD I GO NOW AWAY, AND LEARN TO PAY, THIS KIND OF PRICE?

OLD MAN
END OF LIFE, FLOATING GENTLY TO ME, MERE WORDS CAN'T SAY WHAT
I'LL SEE.

THERE'S A PLACE, WHERE THERE'S NO RIGHT OR WRONG, JUST LIKE I'VE
KNOWN ALL ALONG...
THE LIQUID SPHERE IS CALLING, LIKE ENDLESS BREATH...

GOVERNORS
MUST STOP HIM. DON'T LISTEN! PLUG YOUR EARS!

OLD MAN
BUT TO REACH THAT PLACE THERE, I MUST KNOW DEATH...

GOVERNORS
LOOK AT HIM STILL PREACHING
TAKE YOUR SWORDS.
HE MUST DIE.
END HIS LIES.
HERE'S YOUR REWARD.

OLD MAN
THIS IS RIGHT
ROGARE LOOK
TO FIND PEACE
I MUST KNOW DEATH

ROGARE
THIS IS WRONG

NOOOOO!
STOP!
NOOOO!
[As the Governors kill the Old Man, on the last words, they look at Rogare menacingly,
but Rogare runs out screaming Nooooooooo! While Governors exit quickly audience is
left with the musical question playing: "…Are there no answers at all?)]

END SCENE/SONG

INTERLUDE

(This scene takes place in the GOVERNOR'S Conclave. The following dialogue leads into the first Song Interlude. Music playing here…)

GOVERNOR 1

Every time we kill a weed, another one grows! Does every old man who can tell a story have to become a prophet? And, what about the boy? We don't even know his name?

GOVERNOR

He's nothing to us. We did what we had to do, what we always do…got rid of problem before it got rid of us. We know right from wrong! What we did was right. The boy? He is…nothing, as he said. I'm sure he'll be running from us the rest of his tortured life.

GOVERNOR 2

(to GOVERNOR 1)

It's not like we haven't gone to this extreme before, and don't question what you've done. You were the first to strike, if I'm not mistaken. I was just following your lead.

GOVERNOR 1

I know what you're saying is true, but there is something wrong with us if we don't at least ask "why." Why do they listen to him and not to us? What's so sweet about this crazy message?

GOVERNOR 2

What's sweet about being born from fish?

GOVERNOR 3

I'm not born of a fish! I am human! If there is a god, he's like me, but I agree, we can't go on…silencing opinions unless we have a better plan.

GOVERNOR 3

It's a slippery slope when we start to question our own judgments! It's clear that we know best for everyone!

GOVERNOR 1

　　　Some men are just born to lead, (pause) and others are followers… and what about the women? Our wives for example?

(The other two look at him and smile. He reacts to his own question…)

Right.

GOVERNOR 2
(Taking up the original debate)
They're like ants without a leader. Wandering aimlessly; they just keep coming! We'll stomp them ALL out if we need to…What good do these stories really do any of them?

GOVERNOR 1
We don't want to get rid of the ants! We want to make a sweeter pile of sugar!

GOVERNOR 3
…to lead people in a more beneficial direction.

GOVERNOR 2
What do you mean?

GOVERNOR 3
Somehow we must make it seem like getting rid of the old man was a good thing.
Someday perhaps we can even make him a martyr to our cause.

GOVERNOR 1
That's what I'm saying. What's our cause? What is it that we believe? What's our pile of sugar?

WE WANT OUR CHOICE
ALL THREE GOVERNORS
(Sing first line together)
WE WANT OUR CHOICE!

GOVERNOR 1 (getting an idea):
I THINK A MAN SHOULD HAVE HIS SAY IN WHO HE'LL PRAY TO
AND
WHO'LL BE HIS GOD.
BY GOD!

GOVERNORS 2,3
YES, YES, WE AGEE

GOVERNOR 1 (continues)

IF I HAD MY WAY I'D MAKE IT SO WE WOULD BE AS SNUG AS 3
PEAS IN A POD.
(#2 AND #3 REACTING TO THE LAST LINE)
THAT'S ODD!
…AND I BELIEVE OUR GOD…

GOVERNOR 1 (continues, sheepishly)
OUR GOD WILL BE POWERFUL AND POWERFUL HE'LL LOOK.
WE'LL TELL TALES ABOUT HIM AND WRITE THEM IN A BOOK.

GOVERNOR 1,2,3
WE NEED A GOD WHO WE CAN TOUCH AND SACRIFICE TO AND
WHO'LL
ALWAYS BE ABOUT.

HE'LL BE A GOD WHO'LL CONJURE FEAR AND SUCH, DO WHAT
WE WANT
TO OR WE'LL THROW HIM OUT.

GOVERNOR 3
COUNT ME IN FOR WHAT YOU'VE BEEN SAYING I THINK IS VERY,
VERY
WISE.
YOU GUYS! HA, HA!

GOVERNORS 1, 2
YES, YES, I THINK WE ALL AGREE!

GOVERNOR 3
FOR WHY SHOULD WE BOTHER PLAYING ANY GAME IF THERE'S
NOT
GOING TO BE A PRIZE?
THAT'S WISE…THE PRIZE!

ALL GOVERNORS
THAT MAKES GOOD SENSE!

GOVERNOR 3
WHY, WE COULD MAKE MILLIONS IN PARDONS AND TITHES.
AND THOSE WHO WON'T PAY UP OUR GOD WOULD DESPISE!
DESPISE, I TELL YOU!

ALL GOVERNORS TOGETHER

WE'LL BUILD A GOD WHO WE CAN TOUCH AND SACRIFICE TO
AND WHO'LL ALWAYS BE ABOUT
CREATE A GOD WHO'LL CONJURE FEAR AND SUCH, DO WHAT WE
WANT TO, OR WE'LL THROW HIM OUT.

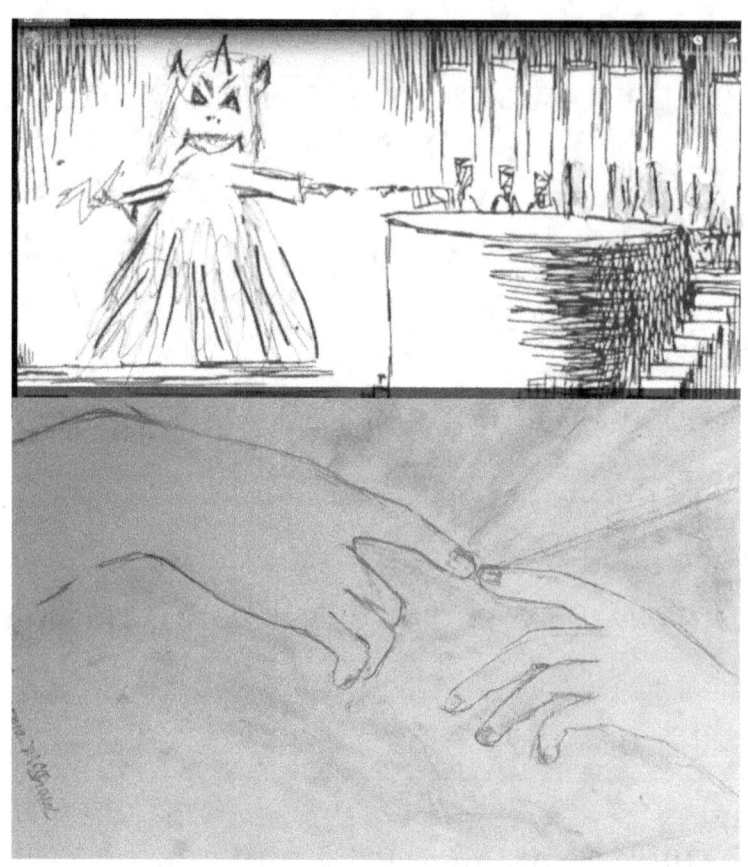

GOVERNOR 2 (emboldened by the others)
I THINK IT COULD BE BETTER THAN IT IS BY TWICE, OR MAYBE
THRICE, TO
BE PRECISE!
FOR MAN SHOULD MAKE A GOD THAT LOOKS LIKE MAN, AND
NOT A GOD THAT LOOKS LIKE FISH

GOVERNORS 1,3
FISH?
GOVERNOR 2
OR MICE.

GOVERNORS 1,3
MICE?

GOVERNOR 2

OR LICE!

GOVERNOR 1,3
I CAN SEE OUR GOD NOW.

GOVERNOR 2
OUR GOD WILL BE LIKE US, FOR GOD SPRINGS FROM MAN.
HE'LL SPEAK TO US IN WORDS ONLY WE UNDERSTAND.

GOVENOR 1.2.3
WE NEED A GOD THAT WE CAN TOUCH AND SACRIFICE TO, ALL
OUR ACTIONS HE'LL APPROVE.
WE'LL BEAR THIS HEAVY BURDEN WE ARE CALLED TO TEACH
THEM, AND TO SAVE THE IGNORANT BROOD!
WE WANT OUR CHOICE!

ALL 3 GOVERNORS
(Conversational, talking over one another)
      We'll call him the Great God!
It's Genius!
Write it down. Write it down!
I don't know how to write.
Give me that paper and scribe tool.
What will we call the book? The Book. Of Course!
Can we wear scary masks and big hats?
Sure! That's a great idea!
(Etc. Etc.—Conversation fades out, as do the lights)

Interlude Continues in darkness or with projected images
(The voices of the Storyteller and the female youth are over the scene of
Rogare's shadow moving from stage left to stage right, perhaps behind a
screen. At the end of this dialogue, an older Rogare emerges from the other
side of the screen, indicating that some time has passed and that Rogare has
matured...)

YOUTH VOICE
(anxiously)
What happened to Rogare? Did the Governors kill him?

STORYTELLER'S VOICE
They would have, had they known Rogare's name. Remember, when Rogare
was asked, he said his name was nothing...He was just a boy so he ran and
he knew how to hide. Eventually the Governors gave up. Rogare, at first

merely wandered without intent, not knowing where he was going. He had many adventures…as we all do…That is the nature of life. We all walk our own winding paths…But, let me finish my story, to answer your questions. As Rogare wandered years passed...

[voice fades as Act 2 action begins]

Act Two/SCENE ONE

(Lighting switches from Storyteller to… Scene II opens with the adolescent Rogare, from the previous scene, walking briskly. Through lighting and effects what

emerges at the end of the instrumental interlude is a young man in his early twenties,

appearing strong and confident. He sings the song,

I'M ALIVE AND I MATTER, solo.

ROGARE
WALKING TOWARD A FAR OUT FUTURE STAR,
WHIRLING TOWARD A DISTANT, HAPPY FATE,
FINDING OUT JUST WHO, AND WHAT AND WHERE WE ARE,
LEARNING THAT THE TIME TO LEARN IS NOW!
IT'S NOT TOO LATE.
FEELING A NEW SUN SHINE DOWN UPON ME.
LETTING LIFE AND WARMTH CARESS MY FACE.
CLIMBING TOWARD A MOUNTAINTOP AGAINST ALL ODDS,
LOOKING, FEELING BREATHLESS NOW AND, I CAN HARDLY
WAIT.
BUT AS I LOOK BACK
I HEAR THE CALLING OF THE OLD MAN'S WORDS.
DEEP INSIDE HE SAYS,
"THOUGH IT MAY SEEM IN VAIN, YOU MUST GO ON."
ASCENDING NOW, THE SKY GROWS BLUER.
WHAT AWAITS ME?
STEP BY STEP, WHERE DOES THIS LEAD?
MY DREAMS REMIND ME.
STANDING UP AGAINST THE STRONGEST FORCES.
CONQUERING THE FOES OF TIME AND SPACE.
STANDING ON A MOUNTAINTOP FOR ALL TO SEE,
ACCEPTING WHO I AM, AS I ACCEPT MY FATE.
KNOWING NOW WHY I'VE BEEN SEARCHING,
FEELING LIFE'S DIRECTION IN MY HEART,
SHOUTING FROM A MOUNTAINTOP FOR ALL TO HEAR.
RAISING UP MY VOICE IN SONG'S DEEP EMBRACE!
MY NAME'S ROGARE! I'M ALIVE AND I MATTER.
I AM ROGARE! LET MY NAME BE MY SONG!

(Rogare continues on his journey and walks into three characters (one woman and two
men) happily dancing and whistling. At a fork in he road, ALL crash into one another.
Rogare is slightly dazed, but realizes that the others find this amusing and are laughing in
good humor.)

ROGARE

You certainly are a happy pod!

INDIFFERENT #1

Pod? You sound like one of those Delphinians!

ROGARE

(a little worried)

It's just an expression I heard.

INDIFFERENT #2

We don't care.

INDIFFERENT #3

Call us a bouquet if you want to…(sniffs the others, frowns) well maybe not a bouquet.

INDIFFERENT #1

(chuckling)

Have you heard some of the ridiculous stories that people have been killed over?

ROGARE

Why, what have you heard? What do you know?

INDIFFERENT #2

I like the story about sharks giving us hands and feet to walk upon the land.

INDIFFERENT #3

Yeah, sharks are great!

INDIFFERENT#2

As long as they don't eat you! (All shake their heads).

INDIFFERENT #1

What about whales?

INDIFFERENTS #2 & 3

(together)
    Too big!

ROGARE

(Trying to join into the conversation)
    What about the Octopus?

INDIFFERENTS

(all three together)
    Too...TOO...

INDIFFERENT#1

(Winding arms together)
    Very...complicated. (all shake their heads)

ROGARE

(Trying to find wisdom in this silly conversation)
    And, while the sailfish IS beautiful...

INDIFFERENT #1

Maybe men just can't relate to beauty.
(All agree with nods, while they look at a close by woman who looks sheepish yet knowingly at the men.)

INDIFFERENT #2

(seeming to realize that Rogare is standing by)
    Who are you?

ROGARE

(Proudly, almost singing...reminiscent of the song he just sang...)
    My name's Rogare...

INDIFFERENT #1

Woa, tone it down a notch!

ROGARE

Sorry, my name is Rogare, and who are YOU?

(They all look concerned for a moment, as if the thinking is somehow hurting their heads and then they sing...)

INDIFFERENT SONG
(Sung by single Indifferent or take turns)
WE'RE UNCOLORED SIMPLE PEOPLE, CLEAR INTO OUR BONES.
YES!
INDIFFERENT, UNOPINIONATED! JUDGEMENTS ARE FOR FOOLS!
YOU WORRY HOW YOU'll MEASURE UP IN SOMEONE ELSE'S EYE
HA!
SAYING ONE IS RIGHT, ANOTHER WRONG WHAT DIFFERENCE DOES IT
MAKE?
NONE!
WHY MUST WE ALWAYS HAVE A REASON TO EXIST,
A REASON TO BELIEVE IN LIES BASED ON A FANTASY?
INDIFFERENT, INDIFFERENCE, THE ONLY WAY TO BE.
POLITICS THAT MAKE NO SENSE, THE PRIESTS BUILD ON OUR FEARS.
A PLANETARY NEBULAE YOU CALL THE LIQUID SPHERE.
YOU'RE SEARCHIG FOR AN ANSWER TO A RIDDLE WITHOUT MEANING.
IT'S THEN YOU WILL DISCOVER IT'S YOURSELF YOU'VE BEEN DECEIVING.
WHY MUST WE ALWAYS SING A SONG THAT HAS A KEY?
WELL I WOULD RATHER SING, A SONG WITHOUT A MELODY.
INDIFFERENT, IT'S-- THE ONLY WAY TO BE.

(The character begin to dance, Flamenco style, without any music, rhyme or reason… while chanting: INDIFFERENCE, INDIFFERENT, INDIFFERENT, INDIFFERENT, INDIFFERENT, INDIFFERENT…)

WOULD YOU LIKE TO TAKE A WALK WITH US? I CAN SHOW YOU THINGS YOU'VE NEVER SEEN BEFORE.
AND EVEN THOUGH IT MIGHT SEEM VERY FAR, THERE IS NO RIGHT; THERE IS NO LEFT; WE JUST STAY WHERE WE ARE!
INDIFFERNT, INDIFFERENCE THE ONLY WAY TO BE.
TO MAKE A CHOICE OR TAKE A STAND WILL BE THE DEATH OF ME.
WE CANNOT THINK, WE NEVER DREAM AND WE HAVE NO IDEAS.
THE CONSEQUENCE OF OUR INACTION MAKES US FEEL SO FREE.
NOW…WHY MUST WE ALWAYS HAVE A REASON TO EXIST,
A REASON TO BELIEVE IN LIES BASED ON A FANTASY?

INDIFFERENT, INDIFFERENCE, THE ONLY WAY TO BE.
INDIFFERENCE, INDIFFERENT, INDIFFERENT, INDIFFERENT,
INDIFFERENT,
INDIFFERENT, INDIFF-ER-ENT!

(After a crazy, exhausting dance, the three Indifferents exit DANCING, leaving Rogare alone on stage, still dancing, but spent. Finally, the music settles down, and Rogare finds a spot to lie down. He is there for a time, the lights dim indicating that night has come, when he raises his head slightly and sees figure coming toward him. Rogare looks confused and startled.)

OLD MAN

(When he arrives)
    Do not be afraid of me.

ROGARE

Who are you?

OLD MAN

I am your friend…
(There is a strange inflection in the man's voice, as if waiting for something.)
    Have I changed so much then?

ROGARE

(Startled, he realizes who he is speaking with.)
    Why, you are…but you're dead! I saw them kill you!

OLD MAN

I am not dead. I've only been changed. Do you remember now?
What I told you is truth.

(Rogare, closer now to believing, rushes to embrace his old friend, but the Old Man holds up his hand, which is rather fin-like now, to stop Rogare from advancing.)

ROGARE

Why can't I touch you? Is it because I'm just dreaming? I thought
you were real.

OLD MAN

I am real, but only here and now, for a brief time.

ROGARE

What do you mean?

OLD MAN

When I'm gone, you will think back on this moment, and you will not
be able to remember it
clearly. You won't know if this ever really happened.   It must be that
way. Where I am going and where you are now are no longer connected. You
must continue your search. You are still human and that's life. No matter
what comes, your death will be the truth for you. I am here now, only to ease
your mind and to show you that there is no further
reason for you to concern yourself with my death. Your journey is not
complete. That
should be your only concern now.
(Abruptly, the old man departs in a flurry of Dolphin Prayer music. Lights
fade.

END SCENE

Act Two/SCENE TWO

(The curtain rises on a new village scene. It is relatively quiet. There is one woman, kneeling, appearing to work near left-center stage. From far left, Rogare enters--older and wiser—Rogare is atop a mountain, far off: Though he is on the stage, he cannot see what is happening here. A woman, stage left, pauses from her work and looks blankly in the direction of the audience as if sensing something. Farther right from this woman another man and woman are lit into the scene. They are within the setting of the younger woman and are the first woman's parents. She begins to sing the next song alone, but each of her parents and then Rogare (slightly, but noticeably older—indicating the passage of time) will also have a moment when they sing a similar, but not exact stanza of the same song. This individual singing will turn to a kind of round, with the four players overlapping and harmonizing at points. The Townspeople are around the others, frozen in various poses until they begin to sing the chorus;the following dialogue is sung by all players.)

ROWENA
FATHER I CANNOT MIND MY WHEEL.
MY HEART IS ACHING; MY LIPS ARE DRY.
OH, IF YOU FELT THE WAY I FEEL...

BUT WHO'S EVER FELT AS I?
FATHER

MOTHER I CANNOT MIND MY LABOR.
MY BODY ACHES; MY LIPS ARE DRY.
HOW SHALL I EVER CARE FOR YOU TWO?
OH, BUT WHO'S EVERY FELT AS I?

MOTHER

I KNOW IT'S HARD TO MIND YOUR LABOR.
SEARCHING FOR ANSWERS 'TWEEN EARTH AND SKY.
ALL OF US BEAR THE WEIGHT YOU DO
OH BUT WHO'S EVER FELT AS I?

TOWNSPEOPLE

AND YET, ONWARD WE GO, DAY AFTER DAY.
WE KNOW LIFE IS PRECIOUS AND BEYOND DISTAIN.
ONWARD AND ONWARD, AS WE SING THROUGH OUR LABORS.
WHEN WORK IS OVER OUR JOY STILL REMAINS.
ONWARD AND ONWARD, ONWARD AND ONWARD

ROWENA

(singing final verse, alone)

WHY DO I FEEL SOMETHING JUST OUT OF REACH?
THAT WILL MAKE ME FEEL WHOLE AND END MY CRIES?
WILL CHILDHOOD DREAMS EVER COME TRUE?
OH, WHO'S EVER FELT AS I?

(In the background we hear the TOWNSPEOPLE chanting)

ONWARD AND ONWARD AND ONWARD WE GO

(Mother, Father and then Rowena singing as a cannon)

FATHER

DEAR ONES I MUST NOT STOP MY LABOR
MY BODY ACHES; MY LIPS ARE DRY.
HOW SHALL I EVER CARE FOR YOU?
OH, BUT WHO'S EVER FELT AS I?

MOTHER

I KNOW THE WEIGHT THAT YOU CARRY,
LOOKING FOR ANSWERS 'TWEEN EARTH AND SKY
ALL OF US KNOW THE WEIGHT YOU BEAR;
ALL OF US BEAR IT TOO.

ROWENA

FATHER I CANNOT MIND MY WHEEL.

MY HEART IS ACHING; MY LIPS ARE DRY.
OH, IF YOU FELT THE SAY I FEEL...
BUT WHO'S EVER FELT AS I?

TOWNSPEOPLE
ONWARD WE GO, HIGHER AND HIGHER
LIVING AND LOVING WHILE TAKING A CHANCE
ONWARD AND ONWARD, KNOWING AND LEARNING
EACH STEP OF THE JOURNEY IS PART OF THE DANCE
AND YET, ONWARD WE GO, DAY AFTER DAY.
WE KNOW LIFE IS PRECIOUS AND BEYOND DISTAIN.
ONWARD AND ONWARD, AS WE SING THROUGH OUR LABORS.
WHEN WORK IS OVER OUR JOY STILL REMAINS.
ONWARD AND ONWARD, ONWARD AND ONWARD...
ROWENA (sings final verse, alone, perhaps au cappella)
WHY DO I FEEL SOMETHING JUST OUT OF REACH
THAT WILL MAKE ME FEEL WHOLE, AND END MY CRIES?
WILL CHILDHOOD DREAMS EVER COME TRUE?
OH, BUT WHO'S EVER WONDERED AS I?

END SCENE

Act Two/SCENE THREE

(Three girls come into scene)

GIRL ONE

(Calling to Rowena)
Hey, Rowena, come for a walk with us!

ROWENA

(Waves at girls, smiling then looks at her mother and father)
Is it all right?

MOTHER

You've done enough this morning; go ahead, have some fun for now.

FATHER

But PLEASE finish your work sometime today!
(Rowena kisses both her parents as she is pulled away by her friends).

GIRL TWO

Come on! Hurry! We all need to get home soon.

ROWENA

Where are you taking me?

GIRL TWO

On a beautiful day like today, does it really matter?

GIRL THREE

As long as it's away from work, that's all I care about.

GIRL ONE

And there are boys there. Let's go see if we can find some working in the fields with their shirts off.

GIRL THREE

I said AWAY from work…I don't want to see anyone working right now. It'll ruin my fun.

GIRL TWO

(to girl number THREE)
You'll never be happy until your married and pregnant, and not necessarily in that order.

GIRL ONE

I don't EVER want to get married.

GIRL TWO

That's probably good, in your case…(all laugh)
(A group of children sing the Dolphin Prayer, nearby. The Girls listen for a moment, then Rowena comments…)

ROWENA

Listen to that melody. Why do the children keep singing that? It seems like something I've heard in my dreams.

GIRL TWO

That's supposed to be a song that children remember from a time before humans.

GIRL THREE

Yes, I heard that some believe that the first creatures were fish and whales, and dolphins and octopusesssss.

GIRL ONE

There are some to the east who try to imitate the octopus, thinking that they should have a hand in everything.

GIRL TWO

I think I've dated a few of those…

ROWENA

Where do they all come from?

GIRL THREE

They're just wanderers, driven from one town to the next, as quickly as they arrive.

GIRL TWO

(changing the subject)
Are you interested in the Bookkeeper?

GIRL ONE

Tell us about the Bookkeeper. I think he'll be a priest someday. When will you marry him?

ROWENA

That's what I was just trying to tell you…I don't know how I feel about the Bookkeeper. It seems like there must be something better out there.

GIRL THREE

Something better than marrying a Bookkeeper? For a weaver's daughter?

GIRL TWO

Sure, unless the mayor, or a priest himself decides to take a common wife.

(all laugh.)

GIRL ONE

Well, all I know that he's expecting you to hear him speak in the square today.

ROWENA

(coyly)
Oh, maybe.

GIRL ONE

Stop it Rowena. When he saw you walking in this direction, he told us to give you the message…

GIRL TWO

Which we said we would…So, don't try and pretend that you didn't know. We'll get in trouble!

GIRL THREE

Just go! Everyone will be there. Maybe you'll meet someone else…

GIRL ONE

Or just come to your senses and decide that the Bookkeeper is a good catch!

ROWENA

I wish I could enjoy things the way you do, but I have dreams…

GIRL TWO

You're a funny one Rowena. You've got so much, and yet you seem to be waiting for something to change. Why?

ROWENA

Don't you ever wish for something more?

GIRL THREE

More? Like what?

ROWENA'S SONG
ROWENA
DREAMING, LONGING,
BUILDING THAT DREAM FROM A MEMORY
TOUCHING, WANTING,
I AM
CATCHING A HOPE FROM INTANGIBLE DREAMS
I'M A CANVAS SEEKING AN ARTIST,
I'M AN OCEAN WISHING FOR RAIN
I'M A WHISPER FILLING THE SILENCE
WHEN THE VOICE I HEAR IS NOT MY OWN.
WHEN SOUND BECOMES A CHORUS
WHEN WANDERING SEEMS HOPELESS
THEN TWO BECOME AS ONE.
GIRLS' CHORUS
OH ROWENA, YOU'VE ALWAYS DREAMED IN A WAY

WE COULD ONLY IMAGINE
WE ARE GLAD TO CALL YOU OUR FRIEND
FOR YOU ALWAYS MAKE REAL OUR DESIRES.
I'M A CANVAS SEEKING AN ARTIST,
I'M AN OCEAN WISHING FOR RAIN
I'M SILENCE FILLED BY THE SILENCE
WHEN THE VOICE I HEAR IS NOT MY OWN.
WHEN SOUND BECOMES A CHORUS
WHEN WANDERING SEEMS HOPELESS
THEN TWO BECOME AS ONE.
LIKE A FOREST THAT GROWS IN EVERY SEASON,
OR COLORS OF A SUNRISE, CREATING A NEW DAY.
MAKING, CATCHING, BUILDING, FINDING
HOLDING ANSWERS TO CLOSE TO ME.
HOPING, DREAMING, BUILDING THAT HOPE FROM A BEAUTIFUL
DREAM
ROWENA….RO…WEN….A…..RO…….WEN…………..A………….

GIRL TWO
So, NOW do you want to go hear the Bookkeeper?

ROWENA
(resignedly)
Alright, fine! Let's go…
(ALL exit)

END OF ACT II

Act 3/ SCENE ONE

(Rogare moves across the stage and as he does, more workers and people move in also including Rowena, her mother and father and the three girls from the previous scene. All are watching the Bookkeeper, politely, though each is still unaware of the other. Finally Rogare works his way across to the opposite side of the stage where a crowd has gathered around a man who is preaching. Crowd is bustling and Rogare is noticeably excited, though he is torn between his first look at Rowena and listening to the Bookkeeper. His attention is drawn away from Rowena and to the crowd as the Bookkeeper speaks.

BOOKKEEPER'S SONG
BOOKKEEPER
HAVE WE COME VERY FAR SINCE THE DAWN OF TIME?

CROWD
NOT YET! NOT YET! NOT YET!

BOOKKEEPER
CAN WE LIVE FOREVER WITHOUT ANY HELP?

CROWD
NOT YET! NOT YET! NOT YET!

BOOKKEEPER
THEN I'll ASK YOU…
WHERE ARE THE ANSWERS TO QUESTIONS WE HAVE?
WHAT IS THE MEANING OF LIFE?

CROWD
WE DON'T KNOW
BOOKKEEPER
WHERE DO WE COME FROM? WHERE DO WE GO?
WHY IS THERE STRUGGLE AND STRIFE?

CROWD
WILL WE EVER KNOW?

BOOKKEEPER
IS THAT WHAT'S TROUBLING YOU?

CROWD
YES!

BOOKKEEPER
YES? WELL THEN, HERE ARE THE ANSWERS!
COME CLOSER, COME LOOK.
PAY CLOSE ATTENTION! NOW, DON'T MISS A WORD!
FOR I'M HERE TO EXPLAIN THE UNKNOWN AND ABSURD.

CROWD (as if confused by he word)
THE ABSURD?

BOOKKEEPER
DON'T BE SCARED!

CROWD (as if frightened by the word)
SCARED?

BOOKKEEPER
WHAT'S YOUR WORRY?

CROWD
WORRY?

BOOKKEEPER
I'M HERE TO EXPLAIN THE CHALLENGING PART.
THAT IS MY CALLING.
IT'S WHY WE HAVE PRIESTS AND KEEPERS OF BOOKS.
I AM YOUR SERVANT, AND WE ALL SERVE THE GREAT GOD, NOW
DON'T WE?

CROWD
OH YES! GREAT GOD, OH, YES!

BOOKKEEPER
I'M YOUR HELPER, AND I AM YOUR FRIEND,
I'M A PREACHER, BOOKKEEPER, AND I'M HERE TILL THE END.
CROWD
IS THERE A SEPARATE PLACE FOR THE GOOD AND THE BAD?

BOOKKEEPER
YES! AND, THE PLACE FOR THE EVIL IS FILLED WITH SNAKES
AND SPIDERS
AND IS DARK AND FREEZING!
(Crowd gasps a reaction together.)

CROWD
BUT THE PLACE FOR THE GOOD, THOSE WHO PLEASE THE GREAT GOD?

BOOKKEEPER
IS A PALACE WITHOUT LABOR… AND, THE SUN IS SHINING, ALL THE TIME, BUT IT'S NOT TOO HOT.
…AND THE WATER? TASTES LIKE SUGAR THERE; IT'S NOT SALTY LIKE BRINE.
(The crowd reacts again and the bookkeeper is carried away by his own descriptions.)
THERE IS NO PAIN OR SUFFERING, BECAUSE THERE IS NO QUESTIONING THE BOOK. ALL ANSWERS REVEALED, UNCERTAINTY GONE.
(He breathes a long sigh then snaps back to the reality of the scene at hand.)

CROWD
HOW ARE WE TO KNOW THEN WHAT'S RIGHT AND WHAT'S WRONG?

BOOKKEEPER
IT'S RIGHT HERE IN THE BOOK! AND YOU'D KNOW IF YOU JUST TOOK THE TIME TO LOOK.

CROWD MEMBER
WE CAN'T READ…IT'S PROHIBITED!

BOOKKEEPER
UMHMMMMM, YES IT IS…

CROWD MEMBER
THEN HOW CAN WE POSSIBLY READ THE BOOK?

BOOKKEEPER
WELL, YOU'D KNOW THE ANSWER IF YOU JUST TOOK A LOOK…

CROWD MEMBER
WE CAN'T READ! IT'S DISCOURAGED!

BOOKKEEPER
YOU'RE ENCOURAGED TO GET WHAT YOU NEED FROM HERE!

(HE HOLDS UP THE BOOK AGAIN)

CROWD MEMBER
WE CAN'T READ! IT'S PROHIBITED!!!

BOOKKEEPER
UMMMHMMMM, YES IT IS…AND THAT IS THE DILECTABLE DICHOTOMY!

CROWD
DICHOTOMY?

BOOKKEEPER
DILECTABLE!

CROWD
ARE THERE PEOPLE WHO ARE THE GREAT GOD'S FAVORITES?

BOOKKEEPER
YES! YOU, ARE THE CHOSEN, THE FAITHFUL ONES. LET ME HEAR IT. SAY IT! WHO'S CHOSEN?

CROWD
WHY WE ARE!

BOOKKEEPER
WOULD I BE STANDING BEFORE YOU? WOULD WE HAVE THIS GREAT BOOK IF WE WEREN'T THE CHOSEN?

(all scoff and shake their heads)
NOW YOU'D KNOW THE ANSWER IF YOU JUST TOOK A LOOK.

CROWD MEMBER
WE CAN'T READ! IT'S PROHIBITED!

BOOKKEEPER
YOU'RE ENCOURAGED TO GET WHAT YOU NEED FROM HERE! JUST LOOK!

CROWD
BUT WE CAN'T EVEN READ! SO HOW CAN WE POSSIBLY KNOW WHAT'S IN THE BOOK?

BOOKKEEPER
YOU'RE MISSING THE POINT! I'LL TELL YOU WHEN DOWN IS
DOWN AND WHEN IT'S NOT. THERE'S NO NEED FOR YOU TO
READ...AND THAT IS THE DILECTABLE DICHOTOMY

CROWD
DICHOTOMY?

BOOKKEEPER
DILECTABLE!

(After the Bookkeeper finishes, Rogare intrudes innocently on the
Bookkeeper, as he is trying to contribute, but does not really understand what
is going on. He applauds, as if what he's seeing is merely a comic
performance.)

ROGARE
That IS amusing! And, you know, where I come from, there are
stranger tales that AREN'T even written in a book!

CROWD
(Together with Bookkeeper)
What? NO BOOK?

ROGARE
(Chuckling, trying to regain the slowly angering crowd's good graces.)
Why, there are some who actually believe in an Invisible Planet, a
paradise of Liquid… out there somewhere… and dolphins are…

(He pretends to laugh, weakly, but notices that the others are growing quiet.
The Bookkeeper gets agitated.)

CROWD
Is he mad? Is this blasphemy! (looking to the Bookkeeper)

BOOKKEEPER
(Taking control)
What other worlds? A paradise other than the one in our book?
What the young won't think of… Liquid Worlds! Where'd you
hear that one?

ROGARE
(Seeing the seriousness of the situation.)

From an old storyteller…They're just children's stories from where I lived long ago…beyond the mountains…
(Rogare points sheepishly, in a general, non specific direction from where he came.)

BOOKKEEPER

(Speaking more to the crowd than to Rogare)
      Umph! Those weaklings! They call themselves worshipers of the Great God, but they don't have the commitment to stamp out this blasphemy! This dolphin trash!
(He points to Rogare, then looks at the crowd for approval. They give it.)
      They let these smiling, slippery fish lovers…

ROGARE

(Interrupting, with knee jerk reaction…)
      Actually, Dolphins aren't fi…fi…fi…

BOOKKEEPER

      They let this slimy rabble run loose, spouting their lies all over creation!
(To Rogare directly.)
      I thought the last of you Delphinians were dead…

ROGARE

(knee jerk reaction)
      But, I'm NOT a Delphinian!

BOOKKEEPER

Why would you deny it? What are you then? And, do you know the truth of the Great Book?

ROGARE

I have no book. I am on the road of life in search of answers. I'm just searching…

BOOKKEEPER

Searching? For what?

ROGARE

Just searching.

BOOKKEEPER

Talking to the young these days is like talking to a riddle-master!

Go away from here, boy. Search for your…whatever you're
searching for…in some other place.
(The Bookkeeper seems disgusted and disclaims to the group.)
That's ALL for today!
(In the distance we hear children singing Dolphin Prayer)

Would somebody shut those kids up?

(The Preacher and the crowd disperse. Rowena is left behind, and makes her
way to Rogare. WE HEAR THE CHILDREN SINGING THE DOLPHIN
PRAYER in the background..)

ROWENA

I couldn't help but hear you.
(Rogare looks startled when he sees Rowena speaking and nods shyly.)
It's a beautiful ideal…The Liquid Sphere.

ROGARE

(Excitedly)
You know of it then?

ROWENA

My friends have just told me stories that they heard from
wanderers. (She pauses then also becomes excited.) They said they
were just fantasies, but you believe them?

ROGARE

I don't know what I believe.

ROWENA

I don't' know what I believe either, or why we have to believe
anything more than we can see right in from of us…
(she is staring at ROGARE and becomes embarrassed as she realizes this as
she says her last line.)
(A voice [or simply some musical notes] calls from off stage…*ROWENA*!)

ROWENA

I need to go!

ROGARE

(Speaking hurriedly but proudly)
My name is Rogare! You are?

ROWENA

Rowena.

ROGARE

What a beautiful name. We must talk again soon, please!

ROWENA

    I…
(seems to change her mind then asks boldly…)
    Have you ever heard melodies in your dreams?
(The nagging offstage voice/musical notes interrupts again)

ROGARE

Why do you ask that? How do you know about my dreams?

ROWENA

Because I have them too!

(Father's voice keeps calling her. She reluctantly tries to leave again.)

ROGARE

PLEASE! Let me see you again?

ROWENA

    Yes!
(She runs toward her house. As she arrives [running out one side of stage and then in from the other side], the voice, now clearly her father's calls again. Rogare fades to the background for the moment…)

FATHER

What took you so long? (mock anger) I thought you were right behind me. When a father cannot find his daughter, he becomes worried, maybe angry, especially when his daughter already was doing her chores one minute and the next…who knows what?

ROWENA

You are angry with me father?

FATHER

You know I am capable of doing nothing but loving you!
(They embrace.)

MOTHER

(Stopping her work and realizing something unusual has happened.

Suspiciously…)
Why didn't you come home immediately? We saw you at the Bookkeeper's gathering.

ROWENA
(Coyly).
No reason, I guess.
(Mother nods her head knowingly.)

FATHER
(Oblivious to daughter and wife's secret communication.)
We should learn not to ask! Do you think that it would be too much for a blindly loving father to expect his once respectful daughter to finish her chores, as she promised, before it gets completely dark?
(To Rowena who is already daydreaming about her meeting with Rogare).
Well?

ROWENA
Oh! Yes, Father. I'm sorry.
(Rowena begins to work.)

MOTHER
(Aside, to herself and audience.)
A sure sign of love is a total lack of concentration. But how? And, who?
End Scene
(Change scenery to depict a place the road from town)

Act Three/SCENE TWO
(Rogare enters, and seems to be searching for something, as a village-woman comes into view, pushing a wheelbarrow. Rogare speaks to her.)

ROGARE

Excuse me, good woman. I'm trying to find someone…

BARROW PUSHER

Huh? Who? (Rests wheelbarrow to listen).

ROGARE

I'm looking for a girl.

BARROW PUSHER

Yes, I'm sure. Aren't you all? (She picks up wheelbarrow and starts to move off, Rogare calls out to stop her.)

ROGARE

But wait! She's a very special girl.

BARROW PUSHER

Aren't THEY all?

ROGARE

(Undeterred)

Her name is Rowena. She's about so tall, has beautiful flowing hair, her eyes like pools of clear water, her voice like singing brook, her physical beauty a glimpse only of the… the…the…the depth of her soul!

BARROW PUSHER

(Interrupting Rogare's revelry.)

A true vision…Nice looker with her inner beauty hanging out… Rowena you say? That's the weaver's daughter. (She points.)

That way ! (again with a nod)… End of the road.
(Excitedly Rogare shakes the worker's hand and then starts to leave, whistling proudly, as if he's just done a great deed. Rogare begins to sing his traveling song. The Wheelbarrow Pusher, suddenly recognizes Rogare and puts down her barrow once again to call to Rogare.)

BARROW PUSHER

(continuing)

Hey? Flowing hair. Eyes like clear pools of water?…Depth of soul? You're that Liquid Paradise guy from the Bookkeeper's speech today!
(imitating)

Dolphins aren't fi-fi-fi…a…a… So, still searching huh? At least now

we all know what you're searching for. Good thing you didn't tell
that to the BookKeeper me'boy. He's got his eye on Rowena as well.

ROGARE

Eye? Really?

BARROW PUSHER

There're are few things you might want to know, before you go off diving
into this whole flowing-eyes thing. The Bookkeeper is a very powerful man
in these parts. Around here, the only ones more powerful are the priests.
They used to be our Governors, until we got the Book, but that's another
story. Here!

(making room on her wheel barrow)
BARROW PUSHER
You've an awful lot to learn about our little village before running off
on your happy way to the weaver's home.

WHEELBARROW LADY'S LAMENT
*Lyrics by Buchanan/Richiusa Music by Buchanan/Gottlieb

BARROW PUSHER (sings)
SIT DOWN HERE, KID, AND LISTEN
TO AN OLD CRONE'S ADVICE
IF YOU THINK WE ARE FREE HERE
YOU'D BETTER THINK TWICE

WE ARE BOUND BY A BOOK
THAT COMMANDS WE OBEY
WHATEVER THE PRIESTS AND THE BOOKKEEPER SAY
AND WE NEVER, WE NEVER DARE ASK WHY

THAT'S HOW WE DO THINGS ROUND HERE
WE WEAR SPARK-L-ING SMILES THAT LOOK ALMOST SINCERE
WHILE WE MARCH TO THEIR TUNE
AND SING ALL THEIR PARTS
IN A GREY MONOTONE
WITH NO FLATS AND NO SHARPS
THEY FORBID US TO SING IT…THE SONG IN OUR HEARTS
'ROUND HERE

HER NAME IS ROWENA
AND LOVELY, SHE IS
BUT GUESS WHAT, THE BOOKKEEPER THINKS SHE IS HIS
NOW, I KNOW ROWENA
AND I GUARANTEE
THAT "HIS" IS THE LAST THING THAT SHE'D EVER BE
BUT LOOK OUT, CHILD, THIS PLACE IS FULL OF SPIES

THAT'S HOW WE DO THINGS 'ROUND HERE
TAKE ONE STEP OUT OF LINE AND GET SLIT EAR TO EAR
WE STAY IN OUR SEATS, WE DON'T ROCK THE BOAT
'CAUSE WE DON'T WANT THE PRIESTS VENTILATING OUR THROATS
HERE YOU OBEY OR THAT'S ALL SHE WROTE, MY DEAR

SO REMEMBER ME FONDLY, THAT IS IF YOU LIVE
FOR BEING WHERE NEEDED
WITH ADVICE WHICH I GIVE

BETTER LATE THAN NEVER
MIGHT SOUND RIGHT AT THIS GATE
BUT WAS OBVIOUSLY SAID BY SOME FOOL WHO WAS LATE
AND REMEMBER, THIS PLACE IS FULL OF SPIES

THAT'S HOW WE DO THINGS 'ROUND HERE
TAKE ONE STEP OUT OF LINE AND GET SLIT EAR TO EAR
WE STAY IN OUR SEATS, WE DON'T ROCK THE BOAT
'CAUSE WE DON'T WANT THE PRIESTS VENTILATING OUR THROATS
HERE YOU OBEY OR THAT'S ALL SHE WROTE, MY DEAR

SO HURRY AND GET THERE
NO DON'T HESITATE
RIGHT PLACE AT THE RIGHT TIME IS BETTER THAN LATE

USE THEIR OWN BOOK AGAINST THEM
DEE DIDDLE DE DUM
MAKE A TRAP OF THEIR WORDS DEAR
THAT'S HOW IT IS DONE
BUT LOOK OUT CHILD, THIS PLACE IS FULL OF SPIES

THAT'S HOW WE DO THINGS ROUND HERE
WE WEAR SPARK-L-ING SMILES THAT LOOK NEARLY SINCERE
WHILE WE MARCH TO THEIR TUNE
AND SING ALL THEIR PARTS
IN A GREY MONOTONE
WITH NO FLATS AND NO SHARPS
THEY FORBID US TO SING IT…THE SONG IN OUR HEARTS

END SCENE

Act Three/SCENE THREE

(Fade in the Bookkeeper re-enters. Going to the Weaver's doorway, he knocks. Rowena's father answers.)

FATHER
Good day, Oh Bookkeeper! To what do I owe the honor of this visit?

(Becomes slightly nervous.)
This IS just a friendly visit, isn't it?

BOOKKEEPER

Yes, Yes, friend Weaver, I come now not just as a bookkeeper, but as one who perhaps might soon be something MORE than that.

FATHER

(confused, like the townspeople earlier)
More? But, bookkeepers are like the fathers of the townspeople.

BOOKKEEPER

More, than that…

FATHER

But, priests and their Bookkeepers are the pinnacles of society. How can anyone hope to be something more than…
(proudly)
… a father?

BOOKKEEPER

That's it! I come not as a father to a father, but as man who wishes to become your son.

FATHER

Please forgive me, but a father comes and asks to be made a son? What meaning, if any, am I missing in this?

BOOKKEEPER

A father has a daughter…(clarifying)…Not I, a kind of father has a daughter, but a father- father such as yourself…he has one.

FATHER

(Still confused, trying to understand.)
Yes, I see…I have a daughter.

BOOKKEEPER

And, if that daughter takes a husband?
(waving hands as if this would help get the father to understand)

FATHER

(Proudly, as if he's gotten the correct answer on an exam.)
…and then, that husband becomes the father's SON!

BOOKKEEPER

YES! Exactly!

FATHER

(Suddenly comprehending what he's just said. Rowena and Mother both come into view to hear the next words.)

OHHHHH! You... want to marry...Rowena?

(The Bookkeeper grows frustrated and indignant, having to have such a conversation with a commoner)

BOOKKEEPER

It is a BookKeeper's right to marry any girl he chooses.

FATHER

(To Rowena, who has come out of the house with her mother and both are are stunned...)

It is an honor to marry a Bookkeeper...

(Again, to Rowena.)

Is this why you stayed so long in the village and forgot your duties?

(Rowena is terrified and shakes her head NO, frantically to both her mother and father...)

BOOKKEEPER

So, if you, or Rowena have no objections... (coaxing a response) I'd like to ask for your consent right now.

FATHER

(Father continues, now to Bookkeeper, noticing Rowena's frantic headshaking.)

I think this needs a little more thought.

(Girl jabs father hard in his side).

No disrespect, but we need to discuss this matter in private...

BOOKKEEPER

I could DEMAND it!

FATHER

Rowena is so young, just a girl in so many ways, and her mother and I need her...

(he responds to goading by his wife).

We don't know what we'd do around here...without her help...

BOOKKEEPER

It is MY RIGHT... by written law!

(Rogare enters now, makes eye contact with Rowena, the father sees the daughter looking at the newcomer and understands what is going on. He speaks loudly and clearly to make sure that the newcomer knows what is being said…)

FATHER

It is your right to MARRY MY DAUGHTER. It's in the book. It's your right, unless…

BOOKKEEPER

Unless what?

ROGARE

Unless there is a challenge for the girl's hand!
(Bookkeeper looks startled.)
Is this not in your book, as well?

BOOKKEEPER

(Seeing Rogare for the first time.)
Ha! You! You would challenge ME?

ROGARE

That is MY right! Is this not also written in your book?

BOOKKEEPER

(He looks at Rowena and realizes she is in love with Rogare.)
There ARE conditions to such a challenge.
(speaks as if reciting from the text)
First the girl must agree to it…I can see that that won't be a problem… and then she must …agree to marry the victor. Next, each suitor must agree to a public duel, according to the strict rules of The Book and the challenge must be direct.
Do you, a mere wandering boy wish to engage a Bookkeeper in contest?
(then to Rowena)

BOOKKEEPER (continues)

And, YOU would accept such a wanderer as your husband over me?

ROGARE

(Both Rogare and Rowena are nodding silently; Rogare then speaks.)
Yes, I challenge you for the right to marry Rowena…if SHE agrees.
(Rowena rushes to ROGARE. They embrace and kiss in front of all.)

Book and Lyrics Gordon Richiusa / Music and Lyrics Mark Gottlieb

FATHER
Our daughter appears to agree.

BOOKKEEPER
(Infuriated at the display.)
        The contest will be tomorrow. Your prize will be your death!
(Father, Mother, Rowena and Rogare watch as The Bookkeeper exits.)

MOTHER
        Fights to the death? What a law! All men are an absurdity! They fear anything that challenges their selfish desires?

FATHER
(Father nods his agreement, then to Rowena and Rogare.)
        Does our…friend and suitor, formerly a complete stranger to me before this moment…have a name?

ROWENA
His name is Rogare. He is on a quest to find his way in life and what matters to him most.
FATHER
It looks as though he's found something …Please Rogare, come into my house. I
would like to find out more about a young man who is willing to die for my daughter or
live with her the rest of his life.
(They all exit into house) **END SCENE**

(Scene Change—OPEN NEXT SCENE AT The Bookkeeper's abode)

Act Three/SCENE FOUR

BOOKKEEPER
(Picks up sword as as he sings)
>Rogare! That dolphin madman! Ha, and his Liquid Sphere
>Ah! But Rowena, like a flower who will soon be all mine.
>And Rogare, a mere child dare challenge me, a keeper of books?
>And Rowena, Rowena, you would refuse me?
>A Book Keeper? A future Priest?
>Liquid Spheres! Ha! Liquid Poo Poo! Diarrhea!

I'LL SING YOU A LULLABYE. AH SWEET REVENGE.
ROGARE YOU LITTLE SPERM, I'LL BE YOUR END

(While Bookkeeper is singing and slashing his sword...)
(...Priests arrive. but as one priest begins to walk into the bookkeepers view he is held back by another)

PRIEST 1
>No! Let's listen

PRIEST 2 and 3
HE SPEAKS OF WOMAN AND REVENGE
Why can't he...

PRIEST 1
Shut up! Listen!

PRIEST 1,2, AND 3
A CHALLENGE FOR THE WEAVER'S GIRL?

BOOKKEEPER
WHAT A FOOL YOU ARE!

PRIEST 1,2, AND 3
HE'S INSANE, WHY?

BOOKKEEPER
I'LL MAKE YOU BLEED.

PRIEST 1.2 AND 3
HE DOESN'T HAVE THE STRENGTH TO WIN!

BOOKKEEPER

I'LL TASTE YOUR BLOOD!

PRIEST 1,2 AND 3
HE REALLY MUST BE STOPPED!

BOOKKEEPER
AND I WILL WATCH YOU DIE!

PRIEST 1,2 AND 3 (bursting in now and speaking directly with Bookkeeper)
WHAT'S THIS WE HEAR ABOUT FIGHTING ROGARE?
A CHALLENGE FOR WOMAN?
WHAT KIND OF PRIEST WILL YOU BE? WILL YOU BE?

PRIEST 2
WE CAN'T ALLOW IT!

PRIEST 1
WE CANNOT PERMIT IT! FIGHTING FOR WOMAN!

PRIEST 1,2 AND 3
WHAT HAPPENS IF ROGARE WINS? IF HE WINS?

BOOKKEEPER
YOU MUST NOT WORRY. I KNOW WHAT I'M DOING.
I HAVE SOME TRICKS UP MY SLEAVE. WAIT AND SEE.

PRIEST 1,2 AND 3
YOU'VE NOT THE STRENGTH AND YOU HAVEN'T THE SPIRIT.
YOU'RE A BOOKKEEPER! AND YOU ARE NOT YET A PRIEST.
NOT A PRIEST!

PRIEST 3
WHAT ARE YOU DOING?

PRIEST 2
STOP CHASING YOUNG GIRLS!

PRIEST 1
FIND SOMEONE OLDER.

PRIEST 1.2 AND 3
LOVE SHOULD NOT GET IN OUR WAY. IN OUR WAY!

BOOKKEEPER
IS IT NOT WRITTEN WHEN TWO MEN ARE SMITTEN WITH ONE
GIRL A CHALLENGE TAKES PLACE?

PRIEST 1.2 AND 3
NO, NO, NO, NO!

PRIEST 3
(To the others)
HE IS WEAK! HE'LL MAKE US LOOK BAD!

PRIEST 1
YOU ARE NOT MADE TO FIGHT. IS NOT THE JOB OF A
BOOKKEEPER...

PRIEST 2,3
...OR PRIEST....

PRIEST 1
...TO GLORIFY THE GREAT GOD?

BOOKKEEPER
NO, NO, NO, NO, NO,NO,NO! HE HAS SLANDERED YOU AND ME.
I WILL MAKE HIM PAY YOU'LL SEE.

PRIEST 1
AND IF HE KILLS YOU FIRST?
WHAT OF HIS DOLPHIN GODS AND TALES OF LIQUID SPHERES
THEN?

BOOKKEEPER
NO, NO, NO, NO! I WILL KILL ROGARE YOU'LL SEE.
SO WHY TRY TO WEAKEN ME?

PRIEST 1,2, 3 AND BOOK KEEPER
ALL THROUGH OUR DAYS DOLPHINUS HAS INSULTED THE
GREAT GOD, GREAT GOD, GREAT GOD, GREAT GOD!

BOOKKEEPER
(to himself)
I'VE SUNG MY LULLABY

PRIEST 1,2 AND 3
(among themselves)
WE CANNOT TAKE A CHANCE.

BOOKKEEPER
I'LL HAVE MY REVENGE.

PRIEST 1,2 AND 3
HE HASN'T HEARD A WORD WE'VE SAID.

BOOKKEEPER
ROGARE, YOU LITTLE SPERM.

PRIEST 1,2 AND 3
(as they drawer knives and swords)
WE KNOW WHAT WE MUST DO.

BOOKKEEPER
I'LL BE YOUR END.

(The 3 PRIESTS fall upon the BOOKKEEPER stabbing him to death)
AHHHHHHHHHHhhhhhhhh!

PRIEST 2
(Speaking after a brief silence taking in what they have done)
> What have we done?

PRIEST 1
(calmly)
> Nothing! We've done nothing.
> Rogare did this. After dark Rogare snuck into the BOOKKEEPER'S room as he was in deep thought reading from The Book. He killed T   he BookKeeper and escaped before we could stop him!

PRIEST 2.3
(pointing to the bloody body of the BOOK KEEPER)
> What do we do with this?

PRIEST 1
> For the moment we do nothing.
> We shall have a restful sleep.
> But, tomorrow I have a plan, as usual.
> We shall *discover* this horrible crime and present the dead body of our beloved BOOKKEEPER to the judges at the contest.

END SCENE

Act 3/SCENE FIVE

(The day after the last scene, Rogare, Rowena, Rowena's parents and many others are on the scene, ready for the contest. The village people have all turned out and there is a general celebratory atmosphere.)

FATHER
This is the hour assigned by the judges, Rogare. Do you feel well?

MOTHER
(Answering for him...)
    He is fine.

FATHER
We are supposed to remain neutral in such matters, but let me say, for
    your and Rowena's sake, I hope the man she has chosen in her heart
is the clear winner.

ROWENA AND ROGARE

(Together)
> Thank you.

JUDGE #1

(three judges enters. They are the same as the murderous priests from the previous scene. This Judge shouts.)
> Let the contest begin!

(then aside to other judges)
> Play along so that no suspicion falls upon us. We'll turn it toward Rogare when we can.

JUDGE #2

> The appointed hour has arrived!

(To Rogare)
> You are the challenger?

ROGARE

> I am.

JUDGE #3

(To Rowena)
And, are you the girl for whom this challenge was made?

ROWENA

> Yes.

JUDGE #2

(Quickly)
> And, you consent to marry the victor?

ROWENA

(as if practicing the words...)
> I...do.

JUDGE #1

Then, I repeat...Let the contest begin according to the laws that have been written by our priests, who speak for the Great God.

ROGARE

(Everyone looks around, at one another and around again. There is a little mumbling in the ranks. The Judges, knowing what has occurred, are bad acting.)

I am willing to fight for the woman I love, but I lack one important element…an opponent.

JUDGE #1

(The judges confer a moment with one another, heads come together, The Book is open and shut quickly then Judge speaks as a spokesperson.)

The rules of this contest are clear. If either opponent fails to arrive at the lawful hour, he forfeits his claim. We must, therefore declare Rogare the winner…

JUDGE #1

(continues…emphasizing mechanically)

…without acknowledging any relationship to the legitimacy of his claim, or of his beliefs, while we wonder what happened to the Bookkeeper...

(There are a very few cheers, but mostly confusion as the judges start to move off very slowly to one side, they are never totally off the stage. Rowena rushes in to embrace and kiss Rogare and the Father and Mother also come forward for hugs and handshakes.)

ROGARE

(Slightly confused.)

What just happened? What happens now?

FATHER

You've won, my boy! Your opponent has retreated!
(Looks to his wife, who nudges him forward to
We need only set a date for the marriage!

ROGARE

(Looking to Rowena)

We have a date in mind.

FATHER

Oh? We do?

ROWENA

Yes, why not today?

FATHER

Now?

MOTHER

(Joining with Rowena and Rogare…)
We see no reason to delay. Our friends and family are all gathered and in a festive mood. Why waste this good cheer?

FATHER

If the priests will consent…
      (pulling them back with his words and focus)
… A father may officiate, then all we need now…

(As though rehearsed the townspeople take on their roles in preparing for the wedding feast and ceremony. This included the setting up of tables, preparing food and preparing the bride and groom etc...
In the background we hear the strains of unseen children singing the Dolphin Prayer which is drowned out by the singing of the Townspeople.)

CELEBRATION SONG

THE MEN
LIGHT AS THE SEASONS COME BREATHING THEIR LIFE IN US
THROWING OUR HEADS BACK WE LAUGH AT THE SKY
COME AND BE WITH US BOTH WAKING AND SLEEPING
OUR DREAMS MAKE US ONE AND TOGETHER WE FLY

ALL TOWNSPEOPLE
AYE! AYE! AYE!

THE MEN
HOPE WILL SUSTAIN ON SHORE WHERE WE STAND
TO SHARE IN THE HARVEST ON SEA AND ON LAND

ALL TOWNSPEOPLE
NOW THAT WE'VE FOUND A LOVE TO GROW OLD WITH
ALL'S WELL IN OUR WORLD AND NOTHING IS MISSING
AYE! AYE! AYE!
I HAVE SOME BREAD
I HAVE SOME CHEESE
WE'LL PICK SOME GRAPES FROM THE VINE

ROGARE AND ROWENA
WE'LL MAKE READY FOR YOUR DAY

NO NEED TO RUSH, EVERYONE'S HERE
GO FIND SOME BREAD. GO FIND SOME BEER.
ONWARD AND ONWARD WE GO.
NO NEED TO WAIT. NOW IS THE TIME.
BRING ON THE BOUNTY OUR MOTHER PROVIDES.
TODAY AND TOMORROW WILL SOON JUST BE MEMORIES.
LET'S MAKE THEM GOOD ONES WORTHY OF SONG
AYE! AYE! AYE...
DOLPHINUS,, DOLPHINUS, DOLPHINUS WE'LL ALL SING
DOLPHINUS, DOLPHINUS WE'LL SHARE YOUR WORLD.
MONODON, MONODON, MONODON PLEASE TELL US
MONODON, MONODON WHAT DO YOU KNOW?

THE WOMEN
ALL COME TOGETHER, THE GIVING, THE WANTING
LIKE TWO HAPPY LOVERS THE EARTH AND THE SEA.
WATCH THE SEA FEED THE EARTH
SEE THE LIFE GROWING
LOVE THE SEA, HUMAN'S BREAST FROM WHICH WE COME.
TOWNSPEOPLE
DOLPHINUS,, DOLPHINUS, DOLPHINUS WE'LL ALL SING

DOLPHINUS, DOLPHINUS WE'LL SHARE YOUR WORLD.
MONODON, MONODON, MONODON PLEASE TELL US
MONODON, MONODON WHAT DO YOU KNOW?

THE MEN
NOW IS THE TIME. WE'RE ALL HERE BESIDE YOU.
JOINING THE MOMENT, THE GATHERING TIDE.

TOWNSPEOPLE
SHARING TOGETHER WITH WORDS OF YOUR COVENANT.
WE WILL ALL WITNESS YOUR GRATEFUL ABIDE.
LIGHT AS THE SEASONS COME BREATHING THEIR LIFE IN US
THROWING OUR HEADS BACK WE LAUGH AT THE SKY
COME AND BE WITH US BOTH WAKING AND SLEEPING
OUR DREAMS MAKE US ONE AND TOGETHER WE FLY
AYE! AYE! AYE!
NO NEED TO WAIT. NOW IS THE TIME.
BRING ON THE BOUNTY OUR MOTHER PROVIDES.
TODAY AND TOMORROW WILL SOON JUST BE MEMORIES.
LET'S MAKE THEM GOOD ONES WORTHY OF SONG
AYE! AYE! AYE...
(The strains of the Dolphin Prayer are a bit louder now from Children still unseen)

ROWENA
FUNNY LIFE, MANY FACES COME AND GO LEADING HERE
YOU CALLED A PART OF MY PAST THAT I KNEW NOT WELL
YOU STOOD BESIDE ME SO I COULD BE WITH YOU.

ROGARE
FUNNY LIFE, SNEAKING UP ON US
WANDERS IN, CHANGING ALL
WE ARE EACH OTHER'S GUIDE

ROGARE AND ROWENA
WE ARE THE COMPASS, TRUE LOVE SOUNDS
HEED THE CALL, I GIVE MY VOW.
WHEN TWO LIVES ARE BRAIDED UNTO THE OTHER
PRECIOUS GEMS DISCOVERED IN OUR HANDS

ROGARE
ROWENA, LOOK! THE CLOUDS ARE PARTING.
ROGARE(continues)
SEE THE FLOWERS BLOOM!

ROWENA
TAKE MY HAND, TOGETHER WE ARE ONE.
AND NOW AT LAST, I AM HOME.
MY HEART IS FULL, MY EYES ARE TRULY OPEN
(the Dolphin Prayer ever present....)
I AM A CANVAS SEEKING AN ARTIST.

ROGARE
LET ME BE A GRATEFUL BRUSH

ROWENA
I AM AN OCEAN WISHING FOR RAIN

ROGARE
I AM ROGARE

ROWENA
I AM ROWENA

ROGARE AND ROWENA
NOW THAT WE'RE WED LET OUR NAMES BE OUR SONG

ROGARE, ROWENA AND TOWNSPEOPLE
ALL TOGETHER WE'RE MUCH STRONGER THAN APART
ALL TOGETHER COME AND TOUCH MY HEART
ALL TOGETHER WE'RE MUCH STRONGER THAN APART
STAND BESIDE ME, WE WILL LIVE AS ONE.
AND WE SING WHEN OUR LIVES ARE BRAIDED TOGETHER.
PRECIOUS GEMS DISOVERED IN OUR HANDS.
WE LOOK UP. WE SEE A SKY THAT'S FILLED WITH WONDER.
THEN WE KNOW THAT THERE'S NO NEED TO WANDER.
YOU ARE FINALLY HOME. YOU ARE FINALLY HOME

ROGARE AND ROWENA
WE ARE FINALLY HOME.
(At the conclusion of the wedding song the three PRIESTS along with
several other unsavory types arrive. One strong PRIEST is carrying the limp
body of the BOOKKEEPER. Walking up to ROGARE and ROWENA
dropping the body at their feet while at the same moment....)

PRIEST 1
Here Rogare! Here is your wedding gift. One that could not be with
us today.

PEOPLE IN VILLAGE
(in horror and surprise voices of Priests mix in with others)
>It's the BookKeeper!
>Who did this?
>Foul Play?
>ROGARE?

PRIEST 1
(sarcastically)
>Is *that* what you think? Could be! We never thought of that.

PRIEST 2
>Why yes! It MUST be Rogare's doing. He does not seem alarmed over this turn of events.
>(The TOWNSPEOPLE continue to murmur among themselves.)

PRIEST 3
(snarling)
>After all don't Dolphins and their like live in a world of darkness and secrecy. Isn't this evidence enough that Rogare snuck into the BookKeepers room last night to slay him as he was deep into his prayer and meditation?

ROWENA'S FATHER
>NO! Rogare was a guest at my home, under my watchful eye all night for obvious reasons, until this very moment. He never was out of my or my wife's sight and could not have performed this horrible deed.

ROWENA'S MOTHER
>Ask the Priests where and how they found the body! So far, the only hands with blood on them belong to THEM!

PRIEST 1
No! The Priests concurred this morning and all agree that Rogare is responsible for taking the life of the Book Keeper.
(Since the arrival of the Priests the singing of the Dolphin Prayer by young children is heard in the background. The singing gradually gets louder and louder.) And Rogare shall pay for this crime with his own. Rogare, you must come with us. (The Preists weapons are drawn now)
(As Rogare takes a step towards the Priests Rowena's father grabs he and pulls him back to the wedding party. The Dolphin Prayer becomes louder and louder, joined by more voices as yet unseen.).

STORYTELLER

(Voice shows that the Storyteller is on side of stage, as at the beginning of the tale)

...Suddenly,

a child came from the trees and stood beside Rogare and Rowena facing the Priests and the Rabble...for some reason, there was a lull as all gazed at the boy to see what would happen next. Some say it was Shark looking down from the Liquid Sphere who was the instigator. He had taken pity on Rogare and was finally coming to his senses about meddling with Creation. He decided to act against the Priests, angry that they were flaunting the gift of life given to them.

Others say it was Dolphinus responding to Rogare's unjust cirsumstances, but all agree that when the child opened his mouth, it was something like a Whale's voice that seemed to bellow from the center of the Liquid Sphere, through the heavens and bathed the Earth....for instead of a child's voice singing the Dolphin Prayer, the sound was almost deafening......

CHILDREN

(One by one more children join Rogare serenely singing the DOLPHIN PRAYER--Just NOTES, NO WORDS. Though the music is explosively loud the faces of the children remain serene and at peace. One by one the TOWNSPEOPLE join in.)

TOWNSPEOPLE
AHHH AHHH AHHH

PRIESTS and ASSEMBLED RABBLE
(in their weak attempt to counter the Dolphin Prayer)
WE HAVE A GOD THAT WE CAN TOUCH AND SACRIFICE TO AND WHO'LL ALWAYS BE ABOUT...
    (Bit by bit the DOLPHIN PRAYER drowns out the song of the PRIESTS and Rabble. We see them shrivel, become smaller as their voices and finally they, themselves crumble to the ground, as if pressured by the Dolphin Prayer).

The scene ends with the Dolphin Prayer Crescendo!

Book and Lyrics Gordon Richiusa / Music and Lyrics Mark Gottlieb

(AN UNKNOWN AMOUNT OF TIME HAS PASSED-- The stage is cleared, except for one small, rather run down hut...SCENE OPENS with Rogare and Rowena, much older, preparing to sing their duet which explains what has transpired from the end of the last act, until now. But first, the YOUTH and STORYTELLER, standing to the side as light come up slowly let the audience know that the present scene is part of the story being told.)

OLD ROGARE AND ROWENA
      [Diligent Sun (DUET)]
BUSY OLD FOOL, DILIGENT SUN,
ONE YEAR GONE, TWO YEAR GONE
WARM, A COLD WORLD.
WHAT HAVE YOU WON?
MORE YEARS GONE,
MORE YEARS MARKING TIME
BETTER WE SHOULD TEND TO OUR OWN AFFAIRS
SPEND OUR DAYS, COMETS IN A BRIGHT BLAZE
FAIR WINDS BLEW ON THE DAY WE WERE BORN
RUSTLING LEAVES IN SWEET DISORDER
CIRCUMSTANCE MAY CHANGE OUR MINDS.
MORE DECISIONS, PASS MORE TIME.
TIME IS PART OF LOVE'S DESIGN
JOINING LOVE'S LIKE JOINING LETTERS
CASTING LOVE UPON DISORDER

(DIALOGUE within music-- [This should take about 24 seconds])
(Two young people come running up. An younger teenaged girl and boy are holding hands, as the boy begins to speak to Rogare and Rowena.)

BOY
(Ceremoniously, and with good cheer)
      Mother, Father, this is NAHIA.

ROWENA
So, this is the famous Nahia. We've heard so much about you.

ROGARE
Nahia? I've heard nothing of this person.
(everyone is quiet for a few seconds, then Rogare continues...)
      ...nothing BAD that is!
(everyone laughs)

NAHIA
(smiling)

I've heard many good things as well about both of you. It's very nice to finally meet you.

ROWENA
It's our pleasure as well, dear...(poking ROGARE)
(Then to son)
But, please son, don't neglect your chores entirely.
(Son departs, conversation resumes between Rogare and Rowena)

ROGARE
Remember when we first met?

ROWENA
And every moment between then and now

ROGARE
Sometimes my whole life feels like a dream.

ROWENA
If I hadn't lived it, I never would believe that so much could happen to two people like...you and me.

ROGARE
From our wedding day onward, we witnessed miracles.

ROWENA
The children's song...just like now. It saved us all.
(In the distance the inging continues)

ROWENA
COUNTING THE SUNSETS NOW
WE COMMAND, DOUSE THE SUN
WHERE HAVE OUR MEMORIES GONE TO?
WHERE DO OUR RIVERS RUN?
THESE PAGES OF AGES,
ONCE DONE, NOW BEGUN.

ROWENA
(looking at Rogare, who seems distracted)
What's troubling you? Is there something still missing?
Did you find what you were looking for?

ROGARE
Oh yes! ...And much, much more....And, yet...
What about you? How do you feel?

ROWENA

Satisfied. Happy. Complete.

(singing continues...)

COUNTING THE SUNSETS NOW
WE COMMAND, DOUSE THE SUN
WHERE HAVE OUR MEMORIES GONE TO?
WHERE DO OUR RIVERS RUN?
THESE PAGES OF AGES OUR STORIES JUST BEGUN

(Dolphin Prayer is played softly in the background. Both Rogare and Rowena clearly hear the tune and react to it...moving off the stage.)

(LIGHTS FADE OUT briefly for set change. TIME HAS PASSED. When the lights come up we see the son of Rogare, alone on stage, clearly still at his farm. He lays down, sadly for a moment, closes his eyes and falls asleep as Rogare did in the beginning of the play. While this takes place two hooded figured approach.)

STRANGERS

(speaking together)

Young man!

(Son is startled upright. The Strangers merely point with a nod when the next two questions are asked...)

SON

Where did you come from?

(Stranger answers with a nod)

Where are you going?

(another Stranger's nod in the opposite direction.)

I...envy you.

(Stranger scoffs)

You find that funny?

STRANGERS

Should we?

SON

(Obvious envy in his voice)

Are you wanderers, seekers?

STRANGERS

(only one speaks))

I was once, but now we are both certain where we're going.

(the two strangers touch hands).

SON

There is something familiar and strange in your voices and manner, yet you are so different from most others I've ever met.

STRANGERS

Do you not recognize us at all, so soon?
(One Stranger removes his cowl and reveals that he is Rogare, in transition. The second Stranger follows close behind. The same is happening to Rowena.)

SON

(Stumbling back, in surprise.)
Mother! Father! Then it's true!

(LIGHTS FADE QUICKLY TO BLACK and slowly rise. When lights come up, we are back to the beginning scene, where the Old Storyteller was weaving this tale.)

YOUTH (a girl)
That is a wonderful tale old man. I love your stories, and the way you tell them makes me feel that perhaps...

STORYTELLER

Perhaps what? That perhaps these stories might even be true! Well the intervention of the First Beings could well be allegory made up to make a   point, but I know that certain parts of this tale ARE true!

YOUTH

How can you? How can ANYONE know such a thing? (looks sad)

STORYTELLER

I can give you some consolation, if you can first tell me my name...

YOUTH

(again, almost sadly)

I'm sorry to say that I've never wondered about the given names of the old.

STORYTELLER

Our names are our songs, and I have one, nonetheless.

YOUTH

What is your name?

STORYTELLER

I have lived here all my life in this village, like you, and am my parents' child. I was named after my father. I am Rogare!

(There is shocked silence among the youth as Rogare gives a mischievious and gentle smile)

 (until this moment the Youths have appeared skeptical, but now all join in as voices from the audience pierce the silence.)

THE YOUTHS AND ALL
DREAMING!
HOPING!
BUILDING THAT HOPE FROM INTANGABLE DREAMS.
LEARNING!
HELPING!
REACHING A DREAM THROUGH A MEMORY.
TRUSTING!
CARING!
LOVING!
LIVING!
DYING!
WE ARE THE WATER THAT FLOWS TO THE RIVER
AND THE RIVER FLOWS TO THE SEA.
IT IS OUR SPIRIT THAT CARRIES US FORWARD
TO THAT PLACE WE CALL THE LIQUID SPHERE
STANDING ON A MOUNTAIN TOP FOR ALL TO SEE
RAISING UP OUR VOICE IN SONGS DEEP EMBRACE.
I AM ROGARE! LET MY NAME BE MY SONG.

[EVERYONE SINGS THEIR OWN NAME HERE}

I AM ROGARE! LET MY NAME BE MY SONG.
I AM ROGARE! LET MY NAME BE MY SONG.
      (Building and building until all voices sing triumphantly the
DOLPHIN PRAYER.)

END PLAY